THE PACT

A Novel By

WILLIAM SCHOELL

Encyclopocalypse Publications
www.encyclopocalypse.com

Third Edition
ISBN: 978-1-960721-97-6

New cover redesign by Sean Duregger
Interior design and formatting by Sean Duregger

The characters and events in this book are fictitious. Any similarity to real
persons, living, dead or undead is coincidental and not intended by the author.

INTRODUCTION

St. Martin's Press, which was not a small press but one of the largest publishers in the country, had begun publishing paperback horror originals and – bypassing Leisure books with whom I had done my previous works -- I submitted *The Pact* to the editor of the line, who bought it, to my delight. Out of my eight vintage horror novels, I have always considered *The Pact* the best, or at least in the top two or three.

Now being published by a major firm with a commitment to horror I thought good things were certainly in store. Alas, the horror implosion that put an end to the first horror boom was just around the corner. Plans to come out with a trilogy set on a sinister island were scrapped, and the editor not only left St. Martin's but the business. I did one more novel for Leisure and one more for St. Martin's before concentrating on non-fiction, including celebrity biographies.

Meanwhile a new editor was put in charge of *The Pact* and after we had lunch and I feared he might insist on several changes – and there was no talk of a new book -- I was so discombobulated that I walked out of a bar without my winter jacket (the bartender kindly ran after me and gave it to me). I was considerably cheered when this editor not only sent me a note telling me how much he truly admired *The Pact* but wanted a second book as well.

As for *The Pact* (which was originally entitled *The Harbor* – after Pearl Harbor -- another case of a publisher giving a book a generic title), I found compelling the notion that the heroine was still in love with her husband, who died during WW 2, all these decades later, determined to bring him back to her when she learns that, in some sense, he may still be alive. I also got to explore Hawaii and its striking and interesting settings, as well as to employ a very Lovecraftian demonic entity, Azarub, who is responsible for much of the carnage. (Lovecraft certainly had his issues but remains one of the most fascinating and influential practitioners of horror ever.)

A more unique aspect to the book was that the trio of main characters are all senior citizens, vital individuals all. At the time I was decades younger than my characters but I suspected then, and know now, that inside where it matters older people are not really that different from their younger selves.

William Schoell
January, 2024

ACKNOWLEDGMENTS

The author would like to thank: his parents, for describing what life was like in the United States both before and after the Japanese attack on Pearl Harbor; his sister and brother-in-law, for sharing their impressions of the island of Oahu and modern-day Pearl Harbor, and for, in fact, inadvertently generating the idea for this novel; Robert Sharpe and John Cavanna for, respectively, mentioning and confirming the Hebrew *Sheol*; and a special thanks to my editor, Jack Caravela.

<u>LIGHT</u>

THE NIGHT has a thousand eyes,
The day but one;
Yet the light of the bright world dies
With the dying sun.

The mind has a thousand eyes,
And the heart but one;
Yet the light of a while life dies
When its love is done.

Francis W. Bourdillon (1852-1921)

For Carol and Tom Altomare
…and the woman who cried on the launch

THE PACT

PROLOGUE

New York City—1941

A quarter moon with the nasty aquiline face of a wizened ghoul or imp was hanging in the sky. It was a cold night, and a rough, yowling wind swept down the avenue outside the Roosevelt Grill.

Steven Russell's wife, Marjorie, twenty-one years old, looking as pretty as Carole Lombard in her white gown and black high heels and heavier, out-of-character makeup, poked up from her gin and tonic and cocked her head. "Steven, aren't you having a good time? You haven't had too much to drink, have you?"

"No," he said. If anything, he hadn't had enough. "I'm just —it's just—"

"It's just that you're going to miss me terribly," she said dramatically, putting him on. She smiled and stared into his eyes.

Her parents had given them quite a bit of money to go out and paint the town red on his last free night before reporting to Church Street at ten the next morning. There was no point in trying to get him home early so that he could get to bed at a decent hour; he was too nervous to sleep and they both knew it.

"Yes, I'll miss you," he said. "How did you know?" He lifted her hand to his lips and kissed it. She giggled. He broke out into a grin, his first genuine smile since dinner.

It was difficult for him to smile, for tonight there was nothing but talk of war.

They had gone to Toots Shor for dinner, had drinks at the Latin Quarter, and danced for hours at the Copa, but there was no escaping it. No matter where they went, war was on everyone's lips. And that wasn't the worst of it. The worst was that those dreaded words "United States" kept popping into the conversation. In spite of his wife's and others' assurances that the U.S. would not get embroiled in this universal madness, it now seemed people felt it was inevitable. "All it will take is just one shove," a potbellied man at the next table down at the Village Vanguard had been saying. He smirked as if he thought that U.S. involvement in World War II would be the greatest thing since victrolas.

What made it worse was that the man bore an uncanny resemblance to Steven's uncle and namesake, the "family tragedy" who had come back from World War I a hero, and literally half a man, the lower half of both his legs having been blown off by artillery fire. Uncle Steven, who'd had such a promising future, was now an old wreck who sat off to one side in his wheelchair at every family gathering, hugging his bottle, drinking continually to reduce his physical and emotional agony. Halfway through the evening he would become drunk and abusive, and he'd be wheeled home by his faithful spinster sister Natalie, who once chastised the others for ignoring the man but could well understand why they did. It was impossible to get beyond the man's rage. It was hard to figure who was more bitter: Uncle Steven or Aunt Lucy. The fine, handsome, young man had grown old before his time, had missed out on joy and love and happiness others took for granted, and now spent his days and nights in a haze of loneliness and frustration.

Steven thought of other people he'd met in his childhood who'd been savaged by war. Ted Rutledge, the news vendor who couldn't stop blinking and smiling, was too brain damaged to continue his promising law career. Barney Owen hobbled about pathetically on crutches and one leg, and was said to be addicted to morphine. That's what World War I had done to people; he could only imagine how bad World War II would be. They said the fighting overseas was terrible, but the newsreels showed very little of the real action.

Steven couldn't even stand to think of it. Of his dying on some battlefield or coming back to his wife with no arms or legs or a mind so stricken by what he'd seen and experienced that he'd have nothing more than a head full of mush. He patted his wife's hand and lifted his drink.

He guessed he hadn't appreciated his good life until tonight: his steady job (even if it was only in his father's appliance store); his pretty, devoted wife (even if she *had* gotten pregnant); their apartment on Barker Street (even if it was shabby). He was entering an unknown world that was more frightening than anything he read in his fantastic pulp magazines (he'd collected them for years until he now had a pile that reached precariously toward the ceiling): *the navy.*

Even now it amazed him that he had actually enlisted in the navy. There had been many reasons for his deciding upon what seemed for him a bizarre course of action, but he had been virtually driven to it overnight. Over the years Steven had been subjected to a constant barrage of belittlement from his father, had been forced to sit in silence at the dinner table and listen to those boring stories about his glorious days in the navy. Steven's mother had fallen in love with Mr. Russell's uniform, for surely there was nothing inside it that could have appealed to her. Oh, his father was a swaggering, handsome man—at least he had been in his youth, judging from faded pictures—but now only the swagger was left, and even that was shaky. Steven's maternal grandfather had also been a navy man, which was why his mother was positively daft for sailors. "You'll look so handsome in a uniform, just like your father and mine," she told Steven over and over again.

"Yes, Mom, yes, Mom," he would reply. It was an annoying litany that seemed to haunt him in his sleep. His mother rarely commented on the fact that her brother Steven had also worn a uniform, an army uniform, and had come home from the war minus pieces. Steven often wondered if his mother thought her brother had tempted fate by refusing to follow family tradition and join the navy.

By nature, Steven was not a rough, physical, or athletic person, and his father was appalled that his son would rather read books than play football. Steven had grown up feeling he was unmanly and second-rate, that he would never amount to anything substantial or garner respect from anyone. He supposed he'd first dug his nose into his books to escape his parents' constant arguing, their chastisement. The three of them would come home from the appliance store the Russells owned on Nostrand Avenue and right away his parents would start in with the drinking. (One day the appliance store would be Steven's; he never figured his life would lead in any direction other than taking over the dumpy shop whose floors, it seemed, he'd spent all his childhood sweeping.) His mother listened to the radio in the sitting room, sipping Scotch-and-soda, while his father went out to the workshop to fix either some broken items he'd brought home with him or something that needed repair in the house itself. He ran gaily through beer after beer until he was too bombed to see straight. This happened night after night.

His father drank more but could handle it better. He would merely get belligerent, but his wife would cry, sometimes over nothing. Steven wasn't sure whose behavior was worse. He would shut himself up in his room and hope one or both would pass out or go to bed before it entered their heads to bother him.

But the night of what he would later call the "Big Fight," Mr. Russell, having polished off a six-pack, had confronted his son in the kitchen. The draft had started—Roosevelt claimed they had to build up an army for defense purposes, though everyone knew he was itching to enter the war—and while most young men would simply wait until their number came up, which was what Steven would have liked to do, the senior Russell thought otherwise. He went on and on about how he wished *he* were young enough to enlist, and that if Steven had any spine or backbone that was just what he would do—prove that he was a man and sign up to defend his country. He had called Steven vile names and made vicious insinuations. "Or why don't you marry Margie, huh?" he hollered, "Aren't you man enough to finally marry the girl? Can't fight for your country. Can't get married. What are you, a man or a—"

Steven had taken a swing at his father for the first and last time in his life. He'd stormed out of the house, near tears, and had walked the neighborhood streets for hours. He had listened to his father's jeers for so many years that he was almost ready to believe them. He knew why he didn't want to marry Marjorie just yet—although he loved her and presumed she would eventually become his wife, he just wasn't *ready* for marriage. He knew everyone expected it—his parents, Marjorie, her parents—but he just couldn't see himself as a husband. Or a soldier. He was beginning to feel so hemmed in, so trapped by everything: his awful life living with and working for his parents; Marjorie's not-so-subtle hints at matrimony—everything was closing in and crushing him.

And it was then that he got his brilliant idea, a way to postpone the inevitable wedding until he was ready, a chance to earn a living, and a means to get far away from that shop on Nostrand Avenue (and, even better, from his father): He would enlist in the navy! It might be months before they would actually call him for duty, months during which his father would have to *shut up* and accept that his son *had* what it took. Besides, he had told himself then, even in the unlikely event that the U.S. did enter the war, he would be a lot safer on a ship than in the infantry, wouldn't he?

He enlisted the very next day, convinced it was the only way. The only way to satisfy everyone's—and his own—doubts about himself. The only way to get free of the terrible pressures of his miserable home life and situation. But deep inside himself, he'd wondered if he had betrayed his deepest ideals, his noblest instincts, just to satisfy a father who was ultimately unworthy of his love.

Steven was a dreamer and a poet, just the type of person that his practical parents could never understand. They were like stoic farmers who could only believe in what they could touch and feel with their own two hands. They had disdain for his fantasy magazines and the esoteric fiction he loved to read, though neither of them had so much as glanced through a page of it. They worried about him, about his ability to get along in the world. They worried so much, and vocalized their worries so often—his father in those stark, brutal terms, his mother with a whining bluntness that was somehow worse—that Steven had eventually become alarmed himself. *Was* he a weakling? A coward? Was he unable to cope with anything but fantasies? No, he was wrong, they were wrong. He was as strong and capable as any other man. Being in the navy would *prove* that once and for all.

He tried to look on the bright side of it. For one thing, he would cut a good figure in his uniform when he got it; everyone said so. He imagined it would somehow make him look stronger than he was—or was that a delusion? He was so skinny ("The navy'll fatten you up, boy," his father said), and he often thought that his blond good looks lacked character and ruggedness. Marjorie had made the mistake of calling him "pretty" once, and he had blown up at her.

Now Marjorie was lifting her glass and grinning. She took two swallows and set the glass down again firmly on the table. She had a determined look on her face. "I know what will shake you out of that gloom. Let's dance."

He was not crazy about dancing; he always felt self-conscious. But he supposed he was high enough not to care that people were looking. He'd felt so awkward earlier. "Okay," he said, getting to his feet.

Out on the dance floor he took her into his arms, squeezed her, and twirled her around to the lilting strains of the orchestra. He loved her, he told himself, he really did. But she had become his wife much sooner than he'd expected.

Marjorie and Steven had been sweethearts practically since grade school. Not only did they go to school together, but Marjorie's parents' bakery was located right next door to the Russells' appliance store. Steven used to chase the pretty pigtailed girl who smelled like pastry around the sidewalk with his broom. She used to sneak him fresh pieces of doughy bread or sweet cinnamon rolls. No wonder a romance soon ensued, one that grew stronger—and more erotic—as they graduated from school and grew older, until finally one night after a high-school reunion they made love in a darkened room where the basketball supplies were kept.

The afternoon Steven went to Marjorie's house after enlisting—wondering how she'd react to the knowledge that he might have to leave her for a long period of time—was the same afternoon she took him aside and guiltily whispered that she was pregnant.

"Are you sure?" he asked her frantically.

"Positive," she said, sniffing back a tear.

"All right, I'll marry you," he said without hesitation.

She threw herself at him and hugged him. "Thank God, thank God."

"I'd never let you down, darling," he told her, though inside he had doubts.

So they were married.

It was a brief, lovely ceremony at City Hall. Afterward they went to a restaurant in Sheepshead Bay and ate fish and got drunk. Uncle Waldo fell down in the middle of a dance and it took three other men to get him to his feet again. Uncle Steven retreated to the corner in his wheelchair and nursed a bottle, while Aunt Lucy glared and looked piteous and counted the minutes until the inevitable explosion. His father danced with every woman but Steven's mother; to the crowd assembled it seemed that she cried out of all proportion to the circumstances, but it *was* her "little boy" getting married, after all.

Twenty-one and he was married. A kid on the way. It didn't show yet, but it would. He hoped no one would do some simple arithmetic, but he supposed he and Marjorie weren't the first couple to get married in a rush. At least no one could say he didn't like women.

He began to feel slightly dizzy as he spun his wife around the dance floor, and led her back to their table before the song was over.

"Steve, where are we going?" Marjorie whined.

Somebody, an old drunk, stopped them in their tracks before they could get to their seats. The man grabbed Steven by either shoulder and gave him a boozy smile. "I'm proud of ya, boy. Proud of ya. Ya do us proud over there, will ya? Show those krauts a thing or two, okay? Give 'em hell. You're gonna go, ya know. The ol' U.S. of A. will show 'em what for!"

Horrified, Steven pulled away from the man without replying. How could he have known he'd enlisted in the navy? He wore no uniform. Had he overheard them talking? Or did he assume because Steven was young he'd soon be drafted? In any case, it gave him a bad feeling. It was a bad omen for sure. *The whole week had been full of bad omens: a disturbing horoscope, uneasy planetary signs, portents of doom and terror.* Steven was in quite a state.

The country *must not* go to war. They must have nothing to do with it. *He* must not go to war. That was *not* why he'd enlisted. *No war.* In spite of his father's and others' ravings, he'd never really believed the United States would get involved; too many people were against it. He couldn't stand it. He would not stand it. He would never survive. It was too much, too much...*What a joke on him.*

Marjorie leaned across the table with concern on her face and whispered, "Honey, are you sick?"

He accidentally knocked over his drink.

Marjorie moved her chair over to his side and sat down. She mopped up the spilled liquor with a linen napkin, then leaned in close and whispered, "Is that what's wrong? Is that what's bothering you? We won't enter this awful war, honey. We won't! Too many people are against it. It'll never happen." She put her head down on his shoulder, but both of them knew, as everyone knew, that it was inevitable. "I won't let them take you," she keened softly. "I won't let anything happen to you."

"Am I a coward?" he asked her abruptly.

Her head shot up. "No! No, of course not! What man in his right mind would *want* to go to war? You're...sensitive, that's all, you—" She shook her head sympathetically. "Oh, I love you, baby. I love you. I won't let them take you away from me and our child. I won't."

But he felt like a coward. He felt so afraid. Just the thought of it. He knew some of his friends and neighbors thought the whole thing was glorious. They thought it was exciting, the notion of going somewhere overseas and fighting the Nazis, seeing distant ports and lots of action. Bombs and guns and bodies. But to them it was all just a game; it was unreal, like a movie in which someone got shot but one never saw any blood. The pain, the death, the sense of loss never entered into it.

All Steven knew of war was old films about World War I,

but what he saw in those films was enough to convince him that there was little "glory" in it. But if he tried to articulate this to his young friends during this siege of war fever, he knew he would be razzed without mercy. Better to keep quiet, to pretend like his pals that he was hungry for action, anxious to see the United States sweep into the deadly conflict and take over.

"Are you drunk, Steven?"

"No...not very..." Still not drunk enough. "I could...I could use some fresh air, though."

"All right. Let's pay the bill and go outside. We can take a walk."

God save me, he thought. *I don't want to go to war.*

* * *

They held hands and walked along Seventh Avenue. Steven looked up and saw the quarter moon—*another bad sign*—and could almost see an ugly and sinister countenance staring down at them. Below the grinning, bedeviling moon, the night seemed alive and frantic. Everyone was desperately trying to enjoy themselves, as if the apocalypse were around the corner; but of course Steven knew that was only in his head. He was the one who was leaving for boot camp tomorrow, not these other late-night revelers.

They stopped for a minute at a bench to kiss. Putting her head down, Marjorie snuggled in his arms. She fingered his tie for a minute, straightening it. Her eyes caught something hidden behind the tie. His amulet. Marjorie humored him when it came to his occult interests; she still had no idea how really involved he was in the subject.

"What's this?" she asked, picking out the brown loop of leather around his neck and fingering the rounded stone object at the end of it. "You even wore your lucky charm tonight!"

"Why not?" he asked her. "You know I even wear it to bed. It's a talisman. It wards off evil spirits."

"What did you say it's made of?"

"Amethyst. Bought it in a magic shop a few years ago. If you're really talented you can cast spells with it." He did not tell her that he swore he could sometimes feel it move of its own accord, hear it humming, see it glowing. Touch it with his hand and feel it give off heat, as it did now. *Another bad sign.*

He was overjoyed to see that his wife's face registered none of the disapproval his parents' did when he talked about his interest in the occult. Though even she might become impatient with him eventually. Since their marriage he'd been downplaying the subject, had put all his bottles of potions and mystic objects away in a trunk in the closet—although he had employed some of them earlier that evening. Sooner or later he might feel compelled to get out the old books and call on *the magic* again. Not that he had ever been successful in casting a spell or calling up a demon before, for which he supposed he should be grateful.

He had been interested in the occult for many years. It started when he read fictional stories about arcane matters in his pulp magazines; some of the stories, written by people with true knowledge, contained references to books and talismans and potions. He had scoured used bookstores in the city until he'd come upon dusty tomes that actually contained the forbidden knowledge only hinted at in the stories: the words of spells, the ingredients for elixirs. It started out as a childish interest and soon became an obsession.

Some of his school friends also shared his interest, but they never took it as seriously. They would perform rituals, make up potions, but they would substitute safer, easier ingredients for the ones that were truly called for; they would enact their rituals in the daytime—absurd!—so they'd not get too frightened. Of course nothing ever happened, nothing ever worked. But Steven was not afraid.

It was easy enough for him to get chicken blood and animal parts and the other ghastly things that were required. Though he'd always held back from really trying something too potent or severe. In the end, he supposed, he, too, was afraid.

"Did you cast a spell on me to make me love you?" Marjorie asked him.

He smiled. He had put a little something in her punch that night at the reunion, but who could tell if it had actually worked or if she had genuinely *wanted* him? "Would I have had to?"

She shook her head. "Uh-uh."

She played with the talisman a while longer, then abruptly lifted it to her lips and kissed it. "There. Now it'll really protect you."

He only wished it were true.

* * *

They had rented an apartment in Canarsie. It was small, but serviceable; Marjorie had decorated it attractively. Now that he was a married man, Steven's parents had increased both his salary and his duties at the appliance store—they could spend more time drinking—and Marjorie still worked part-time in her parents' bakery for a small weekly stipend. There would be enough for her to live on while he was away. The only question was: How long would he be away? If the United States entered the conflict, there was no telling how long he'd be gone, or when—or if—he'd return.

He was tired of thinking about it. Tomorrow he would be on his way to the Great Lakes Training Station in Chicago and that was that. Eight weeks of boot camp. That didn't bother him, though he couldn't say he was looking forward to it. What bothered him was what came after. Roosevelt was determined to plunge the country into a war, was already building his army. It was only a matter of time, no matter what Marjorie and others said. Only a matter of time…

Marjorie came into the living room, wearing only her slip. She was drying her hands on a towel. "Feeling better, honey? Getting sober? We'd better get to bed. You have to be up early tomorrow." She winked. He knew what she wanted, but he wasn't sure he could give it to her tonight.

"I'll come to bed in a moment," he said. He lifted a bottle of cheap wine to his lips and took a good, healthy swallow. He didn't want to get sober. Not tonight. Time enough for sobriety tomorrow.

He checked the glass of liquid he'd left on the living room windowsill, hidden behind the curtain. A potion made up of lemon juice, his own whiskers, water, and just a touch of animal blood. It had not turned color as it was supposed to. Another *bad sign*.

He went into the bedroom planning on making love to his wife for the last time in a long while—if not for the last time ever—but the minute his head hit the pillow he passed out.

* * *

Steven woke up two hours later, snapped awake by the alcohol in his system. He was still high, somewhat dizzy, but strangely alert. He knew what he had to do. *During his brief sleep he had had dreams full of blood and bombs, full of spattered bodies and severed limbs, mindless men and machines. Uncle Steven, hopping around on two stumps, held out a beckoning arm and cackled.* He knew what he had to do.

He clawed at a rabid blotch on his chest. Before going out that night he'd sprinkled a special homemade talc onto his skin, below the right breast. According to ancient lore, if all was well, the talc would not itch.

The talc itched.

He got out of bed and sneaked over to the closet, not

wanting to wake Marjorie. He opened the trunk with his occult material in it and took out several items, including candles, chalk, a book, parchments, and a few small vials. He placed these in a cardboard box, which he also removed from the trunk, and took everything into a room down the hall.

The nursery.

There was no furniture in this room. Nothing. Naked, he placed the box on the floor and bent down to remove some of the items. He worked quickly in the moonlight, determined to do this while he had the chance. There would be no opportunity once he left for Chicago. He could certainly not bring these esoteric items with him into the navy. It was now or never.

First he lit the candle. He drew several lines in chalk across the wood floor, and dripped hot candle wax wherever the lines coincided. He whispered to himself constantly, strange words, old words, words he'd picked up in his readings. He opened the vials and sprinkled the contents of one across the floor, and rubbed the contents of another all over his body as if it were an oil. He rubbed his hands together and then made fists. He looked out at the quarter moon—everything was perfect—and then sat down inside a circle on the floor, holding the book.

He read a few lines, softly, from the book, then placed it open in his lap face downward. He lit another, smaller candle that smelled of incense and then picked up the parchment. Leaning over, he placed one end of the parchment in the candle and quickly threw the burning paper into a glass ashtray, where he watched it blacken and disintegrate. He picked up the book again and continued reading. He was determined to see this through to its conclusion.

He finished reading. The room stank of incense. His oiled body glittered in the light from the candle.

Nothing was happening. *Well, what did he expect? Did he*

actually think that something would happen, that anything would respond to his all-consuming need?

Nothing was happening, dammit!

Or was it?

He thought he saw…*Yes! Oh, my God, it's happening!* There was smoke forming above the candle, a great cloud of smoke, and inside it there was—

The rational part of his mind screamed: *Get up, you fool, the floor is on fire, stamp it out, you crazy idiot, this will never work!*

—a face, the poet-dreamer saw the face and it was the poet-dreamer that the face responded to, the need, the urgency, the *desperation* in his eyes.

The face was ancient and terrible. It was at the end of a head that seemed massive—twice as broad as it was long, thrice as deep as it was broad. It had lips, thick, salivating lips, that had oozing, pus-filled sores on them in which swam thousands of tiny worms or maggots. Beyond those lips were teeth, curled, feral teeth, with edges sharp as saws, and m the middle of each tooth was a portal or hole of some kind that opened and closed constantly like a little mouth. The eyes were very large, with no lids or brows, and the pupils seemed alive with fire. The forehead bubbled with pustules that popped and sank continually and emitted vapor. Steven recoiled both from the beast's ugliness and its stench. It smelled like something that had inhabited a charnel house for centuries.

Steven spoke out loud in awe: "My God—*it worked!*"

He had been successful. He had called up this demon, and now the demon would be forced to do his bidding. It was only the dreamlike quality of the encounter caused by the alcoholic haze that prevented Steven from screaming and running from the room.

"What do you want?" the demon asked in a voice that sounded like a thousand razors cutting into animal flesh.

And as Steven opened his own trembling lips to answer, he knew there would be no going back.

CHAPTER ONE

New York City—1988

It was a scene out of a surrealistic painting, an abattoir and a cemetery combined. There were skeletons, stripped completely bare of flesh, maggots in their eye sockets, lying at the bottom of a dank, moist enclosure. The walls of the enclosure appeared to be metal, and from cracks in the metal seeped blood. The skeletons, though lying on the floor, were writhing about as if dancing, struggling, and in the midst of the skeletons there was one lone man made of flesh, solid flesh, one living man among so many dead.

But no—this man was dead, too. And his death was for some reason worse than the others.

Always it was the same: The man who was alive and yet not alive, would force himself to his feet and stand up in the middle of the skeletons. He would stand up and raise his hands beseechingly, desperately, screaming something no one could hear at the top of his lungs. Then the man would come closer and closer, as if a camera were zooming in on him, and finally there would be just an enormous closeup of his face. The face was always familiar, heart-wrenchingly familiar. But the strangest thing was, when he opened his mouth the widest, it was as if there was another screeching mouth embedded in each tooth.

Marjorie woke up screaming.

She reached out her hand and almost knocked over the bedside lamp in an effort to turn it on. *There.* Light. But still her heart was beating, pounding, in her chest. Still, she felt soaked with sweat even as she shivered from a chill. Still she felt like throwing her face in her hands and sobbing.

Steven! I saw Steven again!

She had lost count of how many times she had had this exact same dream, but she thought she could remember the first night it happened. Over two weeks ago. And she was pretty sure she'd had this same dream almost every night since.

Tonight she thought she would have trouble getting back to sleep. She pulled herself out of the bed and went down the hall to the kitchen. *How many times have I made this trip?* she asked herself. She saw herself as a much younger woman walking from her bedroom to the kitchen to get a glass of milk. Only then her bedroom had been upstairs. Now she slept in the room where her parents had slept for about twenty years, and, in her mother's case, died. No wonder she had such morbid dreams.

Her parents had moved into the house just before their daughter got married. It was a solid, dependable two-story structure erected in the days when quality counted and workmen had pride. Even so, the plumbing was leaking and it was badly in need of painting and repair. Marjorie would get to it little by little, always putting off, worrying about her savings—the little her parents had left her—which had multiplied through interest. She supposed she didn't have to work —she got small Social Security checks—but a person had to do something to fill up the time, didn't she? Also, she would have been far less comfortable had she had to depend strictly on the government checks for her income.

She entered the rather small kitchen with its rippling linoleum floor and butterfly wallpaper and opened the refrigerator. Milk gave her gas these days, so she had to switch to another kind of late-night liquid, usually juice or seltzer. Sixty-eight years of age and she had yet to figure out her digestive system, exactly what made her sick and what didn't, except for obvious no-no's like milk. Her stomach seemed to operate on some random principle that had more to do with its own idiosyncrasies than with natural laws and sciences.

She looked at the ancient round clock on the wall. Quarter past five. It was later than she thought. There was no point in going back to bed; she'd never sleep. She might as well forget about the snack altogether and just fix herself a good breakfast. She had been brought up to eat a full, healthy breakfast and it was a habit she had never gotten out of no matter how much her waistline expanded. Let other women skip breakfast while on their diets; she would gorge herself on waffles and omelets.

Today, though, she felt like having something comparatively simple. She would make herself bacon and eggs with two English muffins and a large glass of orange juice. She fixed a pot of coffee. She had always had a large appetite, except for the period after...after Steven died.

But that was so long ago. While it was true hardly a day passed that she didn't think about her late husband, it was also true that it had been over forty years, nearly fifty, since he was killed. Almost half a century. Why was she dreaming so much about him now? And such terrible dreams! He had turned up in her nightmares a lot back then, when it happened, which was understandable. But why now? And with such intensity?

Marjorie Russell sat down at the table while her bacon fried and coffee perked and sighed deeply. She played with the old gray robe she had worn every morning for at least the past fifteen years. She remembered other breakfasts in this kitchen of ghosts, saw her mother smiling by the stove, her father sitting at the end of the table reading the newspaper. Phantoms. She tried to imagine Steven in this place, but he was never part of the domestic scene. She had never lived here with him. They had shared a small apartment in another neighborhood before his death. Soon after she moved back in with her folks and had never left them, resigned to an eternity of widowhood.

And that's how it worked out, she thought with amazement and not a little self-pity. Forty-seven years later and she still sat there every morning with her parents, albeit ghosts of them. No husband, no children—*no, don't think about Connie, you must not ever think about little Connie*—nothing but memories. She had never remarried. She had told herself back then that she never would, that she would remain in love with Steven forever even if he were gone, but thinking back on it now, she couldn't have imagined that that was the way it would actually turn out. Not that she hadn't had plenty of opportunities to get out of this house. She was a good-looking woman in her youth. But the men always had to compete with Steven, her childhood sweetheart and late husband, and they were always found wanting. She didn't have to tell them so; they always sensed it. She never gave them one hundred percent of herself, only fifty at best. The other half was always with Steven.

Her parents had begged her to get out more; her mother had played matchmaker. All for nothing. All to no avail. After a while the pain receded—there were plenty of other war widows around with whom to find consolation—but not her desire to stay faithful to Steven. No one could even come close...

She was awakened from her reverie by the coffee on the stove bubbling out of the pot. She got up and turned off the burner. The bacon was too crisp, but she could live with it. Time to crack open the eggs and fry a couple. An English muffin, still warm and golden, poked out of the toaster waiting patiently for her to butter it.

As the eggs fried, she took a sip of orange juice. Bitter. She felt grief and stress that was inappropriate as a reaction to a sour glass of orange juice.

She sat down at the kitchen table while the eggs fried and the coffee cooled, and cried, sniffling into the corner of her bathrobe.

* * *

As she rode the bus to work she thought about Steven, which she often did. She thought about growing up with him, playing with him in the alleyway behind their parents' stores. She saw the bright-eyed, freckle-faced lad he'd been when she'd first laid eyes on him and fallen in love. She watched him become a handsome teenager with a sharp mind, a sly wit, and a charming vulnerability she found so irresistible. He was so fanciful, so unusual, so different from the other boys. Smart and kind and full of imagination. He could tell her practically anything and she would believe him. He would make the most fantastic things sound true.

She would have done anything for Steven.

Their parents became friends, even though the Russells were always drinking and fighting with each other and her mother and father didn't quite approve. Still, Mrs. Russell could be very sweet, and gruff Mr. Russell had a soft spot in his heart for Marjorie. Both families bet when the wedding would be: There was no doubt she and Steven were meant for each other. That was one of the reasons why, at that high-school reunion, she had deliberately drunk too much of the spiked punch so that she would become less inhibited and respond more eagerly (not that she wasn't already eager) to his romantic ministrations. They spent more time kissing than dancing. Finally—though she could not remember exactly which one of them actually initiated it—they went into a secluded room off the gym, a storage closet or something, and made love for the very first time. Even thinking about it all those decades later made Marjorie burst out in a smile, feel tingly and excited. He was a wonderful lover. Or was she just discovering that love was wonderful? Didn't make any difference, she supposed. It was grand. So grand she felt not one bit of guilt.

Until the sickness started, the missed periods, the secret trip to the doctor, when her suspicions were confirmed. That awful day when Steven came over to "tell her something" and she was sure he was going to drop her ("men don't want used goods," her mother had warned her), had found another, purer girl, but it turned out he was just enlisting in the navy. "I have something to tell you, too," she'd said, blurting out, sobbing, the story of her pregnancy. To his credit he did not hesitate in doing the noble thing. She was absolutely positive that he was not marrying her only because of the baby, but because he loved her. The baby only hastened things, that was all.

As the bus stopped at the corner and three elderly people, one of whom was obese, struggled up the steps, she thought about the wedding, the reception, the anticlimactic but enjoyable wedding night. The honeymoon at Niagara Falls, where they'd spent much of their time in their room. Her parents had been generous, but they were still on a limited budget. They were too in love to care. They ate out or ordered in and told each other how happy they were.

A while later he finally got the telegram: They had almost wondered if the navy had forgotten that he'd enlisted. But after going to navy headquarters on Church Street he was told he had ten days to report back there, where he and several others would go on by rail to the Great Lakes Training Station in Chicago. Those few days were full of terrible tension for Steven. All everyone talked about was the war in Europe.

Marjorie kept assuring her new husband that it was unlikely, in spite of Roosevelt's attitude, that the U.S. would get involved, that he'd ever have to enter the conflict, but Steven could not stop worrying. *And of course he'd been right all along.*

Though there was a pall hanging over the evening that even the dancing, the food, the alcohol could not entirely dissipate, they had a wonderful time the night before he had to go to Chicago, the last time she ever saw him. He got depressed, quiet, now and then throughout the evening, but generally he had fun. She hoped he had fun. She remembered how they'd taken a walk, and he got drunk, and passed out before he could make love to her. When she got up in the morning, hung over and bleary-eyed, he was gone. Gone. He had probably tried to wake her, but she'd been too tired. She could have kicked herself. At least he left behind a sweet note for her to read, a cryptic message telling her not to worry, that no matter what happened, war or no war, he was *sure* he would be safe. She got out of bed and wondered why the apartment smelled of incense. In the nursery—*don't think about little Connie!*—there were strange markings on the floor that had been insufficiently erased, as well as a couple of melted candles. And a stench that still lingered long after she had aired the room out for a week.

He wrote to her and phoned her from boot camp. He had a weekend leave after the sixty days of basic training were up, but it was hardly enough time for either of them to travel to the other. Then he was sent even farther away, to the replacement center at the San Diego Naval Station. He had another, longer leave out in California, but the price of flying was too prohibitive; her parents offered to lend her, sacrifice, the money, but she refused, something for which she'd never quite forgiven herself. Maybe she might have somehow changed things, affected time, in some small but pivotal way, had she gone.

He wrote to tell her that he was being assigned to the

U.S.S. *Arizona* in Pearl Harbor as a seaman, first class. She still had the note: "I won't be a big shot, that's for certain. I'll just be chipping paint, cleaning up. Help load the ship. Maybe K.P. if I'm not careful. Who said this was better than the army?"

The bus was nearing her stop. She refused, *refused*, to cry in public and become a spectacle for the uncaring strangers all around her, the sullen youths, the mean-faced workmen, the brightly dressed young yuppie wives. But in her heart she thought: *Steven, we both broke our promises. I didn't protect you and you didn't protect yourself.*

As usual, she felt desolate.

* * *

Marjorie's parents had sold their bakery only a few years after the end of the war. She had taken a variety of odd jobs ever since, mostly in shops and small businesses of one sort or another. She had worked as a supermarket check-out clerk for a while, but the work was too rushed and impersonal for her tastes. Marjorie liked to be able to talk to people, to get to know her customers, at least in a casual way. She got tired of all the strangers in the supermarkets. (Even the ones who came in repeatedly were strangers.) The people she worked with were too young: teenagers, snotty kids, who seemed to speak a different language. She hated it.

She had had this job at Melvin's butcher shop for the past eight years. Now that all the big supermarket chains were opening their own delicatessens and sandwich shops, the smaller butcher shops were quickly becoming a thing of the past, but Melvin's had been a staple of his neighborhood for twenty-five years. They offered quality meat at reasonable prices, and in recent years had branched out to compete with the mini-marts and delis, offering sandwiches, a variety of salads, small grocery items. Melvin himself was a grouchy but likable fifty-eight-year-old who spoke abruptly to his customers (Marjorie provided the soft touch), but never kept them waiting. He liked Marjorie, she knew, and respected her. She gave a good day's work and never complained. Marjorie's salary was nothing to write home about, but it was adequate. She was on her feet most of the day, but at least, she told herself, she would make the extra money she might need to have a nice meal in a fancy restaurant now and then (with whom?), go away for a two-week vacation every year (but with whom?), and make sure she always had a brand-new TV set every seven years or so, so she could watch all her favorite programs (by herself). Then there were all the gifts she'd buy for nonexistent nieces and nephews.

She had to face it: Whatever her financial needs, she worked primarily because she was lonely.

"Hello, dear," Melvin said when she walked in the door. The place had a wonderful smell. It was small, though, with just a narrow strip of space between the far wall and the counter for the customers to stand in. Melvin had put shelves on the wall, making the place more cramped, and there was a new freezer in back containing ice cream, ice cubes, and some frozen TV dinners.

Melvin stood there by the cash register with his bloodied apron on. He wore a gray shirt and brown pants. He waddled when he walked due to his girth, which ballooned every year. He had no hair except for a gray fringe on the sides and back, a clean-shaven pudgy little face that was oddly boyish, and was only about five-feet-four with his shoes on. He had thick, homely features but was nevertheless "cute" in that certain fashion. He needed a haircut in back where the hairs curled up greasily away from his collar.

Marjorie put on her apron and got another cup of coffee from the machine that she would later use to pour coffee-to-go for fifty cents a shot. Melvin's son, Barry, came out of the back room, even bloodier than his father, to get some coffee and say hello. Barry spent most of his time cutting up meat in the back, while Marjorie waited on customers and tended to the cash register. Melvin would slice up the bologna and measure out the potato salad, and either assist his son or Marjorie, depending on whoever needed him. All three of them kept so busy—there were very few slow periods—that the eight hours went by at a rapid pace.

Quite a few of the customers were regulars. Marjorie had her favorites. There was Mrs. Bronson, who came in and told her about the adventures of her three college-age daughters who went on dates with rich, successful men in Manhattan. And Mr. Pollack, the eighty-year-old widower who came in every Monday without fail for a liverwurst sandwich that he would eat at home while poring over the latest *TV Guide* and circling late shows, which, he confided, he never actually had the energy to stay up to see. Then there were: Lulu Turner, a playful overweight woman who regaled Marjorie with tales of her latest disastrous diet; Mrs. Abbott, who had recently married and was now expecting; and Mrs. Henry, who brought her two adorable children into the store with her, where Marjorie would sometimes give them pieces of complimentary sausage.

Marjorie thought of these people as her friends, but they weren't really. She lived vicariously through them, just as most of them lived vicariously through their children or other relatives. They would tell her about the weddings, the births and deaths and dinner parties, but Marjorie was never invited, never took part; not that she expected to. She was only a clerk, after all, not a close friend. Still, they were the only "family" she had.

She often wondered where all her friends had gone. Seemed to her she'd had quite a few when she was younger, before she was married. She was always popular in high school—or was that just an illusion? Just because people were friendly to you, liked you, didn't mean they felt close to you.

She always had trouble telling the difference. It was nobody's fault, just the way things were. She supposed after Steven's death, after she ran back home to Mommy and Daddy and shut herself away from the world, her friends, her real friends, lost patience with her after a while. She would never go out on a date, not even after a couple of years had passed. "You're not the only one who lost a husband in the war," someone once snapped at her. *He wasn't just my husband,* she would think, *he was Steven.*

And of course there was Connie...She supposed some people disapproved. *No, you mustn't think about Connie!*

Steven's death changed her, the war changed her, as it had so many people. But whereas most people recovered, at least to some degree, Marjorie never got over it. She would only get so close to people, both men and women, then start backing off, breaking dates, making excuses. Oh, she did have a few girl friends over the years, confidantes and lunch partners, but she never got too close to them, and usually when they got married she let them drift away. She had outlived whoever she had become comparatively close to in middle age. She wasn't really close to anyone now; she had a few friendly neighbors, dear people who were kind to her but had their own lives to live, a few older acquaintances she saw now and then for simple companionship, but ever since that first great tragedy of her life, the death of her husband, Marjorie felt no love, no passion, no desperate need for, or attachment to, anyone.

"Push the coleslaw," Melvin said to her out of the corner of his mouth as he sharpened a knife. "It's going slow and I don't want to have to throw it all out."

She laughed. "Okay." She'd mention the slaw to every customer the same way the little girls at McDonald's around the corner always asked "Have some fries or apple pie with your burger?" during her infrequent lunches there. "Have some coleslaw with your barbecued chicken, Mrs. Finster?"

The morning went quickly, as usual, and before she knew it she was on her way to a small restaurant on Paul Street for lunch. Of course she could always have a snack at the butcher shop, but she felt it was healthy and uplifting for her to get away from her place of employment for a little while, have some different kind of food, even pizza, and then take a brisk walk afterward to aid her digestion.

She was about to turn into a small Chinese place for one of their special chow mein-and-egg roll lunches when she heard someone behind her calling her name. "Marjorie. Marjorie. Wait up! Wait up!"

She turned around, wondering who it could be.

There was a man waving his arms and running—actually walking in a fast and awkward manner—in her direction. He looked familiar, something about the face, the expression, the arms waving frenetically in the air.

It was...it was Steven.

Steven, her dead husband.

She grew dizzy; *she saw a flash of skeletons and rotting bodies, a widening mouth with teeth inside it, and on the teeth, more open mouths; saw upraised, beseeching arms. Steven, Steven...She felt faint, started to sway to the side, began to topple.*

Strong arms grabbed her, prevented her from falling. She was led over to a bench at the bus stop, held up, then gently pushed down to a sitting position. Grateful. So grateful to the Good Samaritan. Her memory returned from the haze where it had receded. *Steven.*

"Steven—"

She looked up. No, it wasn't Steven. It was a man she knew. It was the man who had called her name, who had waved at her. There never had been any Steven. It was all in her mind. What was the matter with her? Was she going crazy?

"Are you all right, Marjorie?" the man asked. He smiled. "I haven't had a woman swoon at the sight of me in years."

His name was Charles Emerall and he was also in his sixties. He came to the butcher shop frequently and was always flirting playfully with Marjorie. She didn't know if he was a widower, a bachelor, or even if he was still married. She knew he wanted to know her better, but so far she had resisted him.

When she felt better he took her into the Chinese restaurant and they sat at a table. "I'm going to buy you lunch," he told her firmly, "after frightening you that way. You say you thought I was someone else. Who?"

She hesitated for quite a while. The silence grew uncomfortable and she felt embarrassed. She had to say something. Finally, it came out: "Steven. Uh…that's my late husband."

He seemed concerned. "Yes. Melvin at the butcher shop told me you were a widow. It must have been a great shock." His hand reached out and patted hers; it lingered, squeezing and massaging her fingers.

She pulled the hand away.

He frowned. "Do you find me that repulsive, Marjorie?"

"No," she said. "It's just that…well, I think you should know."

He cocked his head curiously.

"I think my husband is alive," she said.

CHAPTER TWO

Charles was looking at her with a strange mixture of confusion and anxiety on his face. His lower lip trembled. "You think your husband is still alive?" He blinked. "I'm sorry. I must have misunderstood Melvin. He said your husband died in the war." His eyes lit up for a moment. "Ah, I see. I guess his body was never recovered, is that it?" His brow furrowed as if to suggest concern and to apologize for the indelicacy of the remark.

Marjorie nodded slightly, but inside she didn't know what she was thinking or what she was saying. What had possessed her to say such a thing? Even if for some reason her husband hadn't been on his ship when it was bombed, that would not explain why he had never contacted her or come home to her. She had accepted—more or less—his death years ago. Why was she so convinced he was alive?

"Has something happened recently to make you believe he's still living? It must be very troubling to you—after all these years..."

"Yes, yes, it is troubling." She stopped short when the waitress came by to hand them their menus. They remained unopened on the tabletop. "Actually," she continued once the waitress had retreated, "it's not so much that Steven, my husband, is *alive*, as that he's…well, I feel he's trying to get a message to me, or…" She shrugged. "I can't explain it, Mr. Emerall."

"Charles, please."

"Charles." Her hand went up and rubbed her forehead. "I don't know quite *what* I mean. I know that my husband is dead. At least I think I do. But these past two weeks—it's as though he's never out of my mind. More so than usual, I mean. I always think about him, but now I don't even *have* to think about him—it's as though he's *there*, inside my head, all the time. Maybe I *am* going crazy."

He touched her hand with his own again and this time she didn't pull back. "Not at all. Things like this can happen. Take my word for it. You're not going crazy. Sometimes the dead" —he hesitated, as if wondering how much she could take— "the dead can reach out to us. Perhaps that's what is happening."

Marjorie pressed her fingers against her lips for a moment, then removed them. "I see him in dreams," she said softly. "The same terrible dream, over and over. He's trying to reach me, trying to tell me something, warn me of something." She shook her head and sighed. "I'm sorry to bother you with this. You must think I'm a batty old woman."

"Not at all. Please continue. I'm interested." He squeezed her hand reassuringly.

"And just now—thinking you were Steven. Why, it doesn't even make sense. You look nothing like him. It's as if it was a vision or something."

"There may be a reason why you thought *I* was your husband. I study dreams," he told her, "and omens and fore-warnings. It's my work. At the butcher shop once or twice during the past couple of weeks I sensed how troubled you were, how preoccupied. I wanted to help you, and perhaps I can. Perhaps you can tell me more about these dreams of yours, and I can interpret them for you."

The impatient young waitress came over and asked if they were ready to order. Charles opened his menu and smiled apologetically. "Give us a few minutes more," he said. His eyes studied the items on the menu. "The chicken with broccoli is very good here," he told her. "I recommend it."

"Oh?" She opened the menu and pretended to read it, but her eyes were on him. He was a pleasant, friendly man she'd first seen in the butcher shop over two years ago. They often conversed. He had a strong face with a large, almost aquiline nose and a small mouth. She'd always thought he bore a resemblance to the old actor Paul Henreid, who'd lit the two cigarettes for Bette Davis in an old movie whose name she could never recall. He had a European accent like Henreid, too, though it was not as smooth and romantic—a bit higher and choppier, more like Lawrence Welk's but not as caricatured.

She liked Mr. Emerall, found him attractive, but he scared her, too. He was so sophisticated in his manner and his speech. And what was she but a dowdy Brooklyn frump? She didn't know what he saw in her, if anything. And sitting there in her plain cotton dress, which was neat and clean and cool but nothing like the handsome summer suit he had on, she suddenly felt quite awkward and embarrassed. She panicked. What was she doing here? Why had she been telling him such personal things? Why had she confused him, even momentarily in the sunlight's glare, with Steven? The gentleman probably thought she was hinting that she wanted to marry him. This was humiliating.

"What will you have, Marjorie?" he asked her, putting down his menu.

She dropped hers onto the table. "Nothing. I mean…this is very nice of you…but," she lied, "it's already past my lunch hour. I'll get in trouble when I get back. I don't know what I was thinking of when I accepted your invitation."

"Oh? I thought you were heading for here when I saw you on the street."

"Probably just wanted to look at the menu, I guess. For future reference." She giggled. She got to her feet. "I'm so sorry. I forgot what time it was. Please forgive me; I feel so silly. I just don't want to get fired, you understand."

Charles wore an expression of infinite patience. "I don't think Melvin will fire you. If he does, I'll take my business elsewhere."

She said, "Perhaps we can have lunch some other day. And I'm sorry about leaving so abruptly."

"Fine. I'll take a rain check. And don't worry—I eat here by myself quite frequently."

"Thanks." She started to turn away, when he motioned for her to stop and pulled out his wallet. He gave her a card. "Call me sometime. Perhaps I can help." Seeing her puzzled expression, he added, "With those dreams of yours, that is."

Outside on the sidewalk, she stopped to study the card.

Charles Emerall, it read. Private and Spiritual Investigations.

Marjorie was inclined to throw it immediately in the trash bin, but something told her to hold on to it. Before long, she mused, she might require the odd Mr. Emerall's services.

* * *

The afternoon went by quickly, and soon she was back on the bus heading home.

On the bus there was nothing to keep her mind occupied. She rarely read papers because they depressed her, and it was impossible to flip the pages of one on the crowded bus anyway without its getting crushed and sloppy. She would look out the windows but she had practically every corner, bus stop, house, shrub, and mom-and-pop grocery store memorized. How many times had she taken this bus, back and forth, back and forth, a half hour of her life at a time, something to fill the void, the emptiness of her existence? Even this boring bus ride was better than nothing.

They went past the middle-class Brooklyn neighborhoods with which she was most familiar. Along the avenue the district was almost entirely commercial; on each side street there were one- or two-story homes, sometimes two-family houses, with very small lawns and back yards and a few little kids dragging tiny wagons and dogs behind them. Every street was just like her own. The people she saw were lower-middle-class: not poor by any means, but not wealthy enough to be satisfied. Scrimping and saving, scrimping and saving, to get the cars, the coats, the clothes, the college educations, the "necessities," such as VCR's, that everyone seemed to go for these days. Marjorie didn't own a VCR. Her TV set and her old record player were all that she needed; this newfangled stuff that broke down after two years or less just didn't interest her. The world had changed so much.

And Steven, you didn't see any of it. You didn't see the men walk on the moon. You haven't seen the new hairstyles, the short skirts on women that you probably would have loved. Presidents resigning, assassinations. Wild flashy cars and rock stars. Even an old bag like her had heard of Elvis and The Beatles—they were "old hat" these days—and she realized with a bit of a shock that Steven even predated *them.* He had missed it all, the good and the bad. Civil rights. Feminism. Watergate. (She did watch the news on TV now and then, though she could hardly be called a political creature.) Medical breakthroughs. (*Artificial hearts, Steven, imagine that!*) Nuclear bombs, Cinerama, frozen dinners, television—Lord, Steven never knew television! Never saw "I Love Lucy" or "The Honeymooners." Never knew who Marilyn Monroe was, or Jayne Mansfield. Never ate at Burger King or heard the term "fast food." Hot rods, Yo-yos, Hula Hoops. Long hair on boys. Army jackets on girls.

Demonstrations. Vietnam. Copy machines and computers. *Everything today is computers, Steven; they have everything about you on little screens that light up when you press a button. Kids play with word processors instead of toys.*

During each new amazing development since the war years, she supposed that she must have wondered at the time what Steven would think about it. But now it just seemed as if he had missed everything, and she had forgotten to share it all with his memory. *What a strange world you'd find it, Steven; not really a nice world.* The crime, and the hate between races, and the strange people and languages flooding into the city. New York had changed. *You have to lock your doors at night now, imagine that.* Drug addicts on every corner. Muggers. Yet in some ways the world wasn't that different. In some ways it was still the same: Loneliness was the very worst thing of all.

And at the thought of loneliness her mind was dragged back over forty years to the Sunday afternoon when her parents held a cocktail party and dinner for some of the neighbors. Steven's parents had come, but only she and her parents paid them any attention. As usual, they drank too much and argued too loudly and were soon not speaking to each other...

Marjorie, newly wed, sat on the sofa sipping sarsaparilla and wondered what she could do to keep the Russells from ruining her parents' party. The Russells could be so coarse and they always drank too much. Most people forgot that Marjorie's parents and Steven's parents had known one another for years and assumed the Russells had been invited because Marjorie was married to their son. The other guests at the party were polite—the Russells were Marjorie's in-laws, after all—but did their best to avoid them.

Staggering, full of too many beers, Mr. Russell came over and practically fell onto her lap. She pushed him aside gently and he winked at her. "Steven doesn't know what he's missin', does he, girlie?"

She smiled politely, but wished he'd either pass out or go

home. She looked over at Mrs. Russell and saw her mother-in-law watching the whole scene with disapproval.

"Got a kiss for your daddy, huh? A kiss?"

"Mr. Russell," she said, "you're not my daddy, you're my father-in-law."

"Ahh." He puckered his lips distastefully and loomed in toward her. She could smell his breath, hot and unpleasantly pungent. "Don't be like that. I'm your daddy, too, now. Daddy Russell. And"—he winked—"what Steven can't do for ya, your new daddy can."

"Mr. Russell, *please!*"

"*Does* he please ya, huh? Does he satisfy ya? Can he satisfy ya, that numbskull son of mine? Surprised the army even took him."

"He's in the navy, Mr. Russell." She was desperate for him to get away from her.

"Who cares?" Russell was so drunk he could barely talk. " 'Nuff 'bout that queer. Give us a kiss, huh? Just one kiss?"

Suddenly his face was yanked away from Marjorie's and he winced. Mrs. Russell, standing over them, lifted her husband's head up by his hair. The guests tried to look in every direction but over at the sofa.

Marjorie was mortified. As her two parents-in-law struggled, Mrs. Russell's drink spilled out of her glass and onto Marjorie's dress. Mr. Russell reached up and gave his wife a hard slap. Mrs. Russell howled in anger and started batting him on the head. The glass flew out of her hand and hit the baseboard. They sounded like a couple of alley cats. Marjorie's father came over and tried to quiet the two of them, but Mrs. Russell nearly clawed him.

Finally her mother came over and scolded them in that stern but womanly way of hers. "Cut it out or I'll have to ask you to leave."

Mrs. Russell looked insulted. *Is that any way to talk to your son-in-law's parents?* she seemed to be thinking.

Mr. Russell murmured under his breath, "Bitch!"

As usual, Marjorie's gentle father tried to apologize for them. "They had too much to drink."

It was a terrible, awkward moment and Marjorie wanted to die.

But it was all forgotten when the front door opened and the Andersons' teenaged son, Paul, who'd been next door minding his sister, Kathy, rushed in to say, "It's on the radio! It's on the radio! The Japs just bombed Pearl Harbor!"

Marjorie froze. She felt sick and numb and her heart was beating so fast it was as if it would wear itself out in a minute.

Everyone spoke at once.

"Pearl Harbor," her mother said. "Isn't that where...?"

"Those sneakin', dirty Japs!"

"It's gonna be war," someone said. "War's for certain."

Marjorie was appalled. War. No! Not war. She had promised Steven. Steven mustn't go to war. She didn't want her husband to die.

And then she realized how pathetic her concern truly was: Paul had said the Japanese had *bombed* Pearl Harbor.

Steven might *already* be dead.

She jumped up into her mother's arms. "Mommy, Mommy. No. *No.* I just got married. I just got married." She didn't care who heard or who knew: "I'm gonna have a baby." Her face erupted into tears. "My God, Steven! *Steven!*"

His face pale, frightened by her outburst, young Paul dashed back out the front door, where his parents followed to listen to their radio. All thoughts of dinner were forgotten. Marjorie heard her father trying to tell the foolishly drunken Russells what had happened. *Are you satisfied now?* she screamed at them inside her head. *Are you glad that Steven might have been killed?*

"There, now," her mother consoled her. "Wait until we have more information. I'm sure Steven's all right. There's a big naval station there, honey. They'd knock those planes right out of the sky. Maybe no one was hurt at all. Maybe just a few buildings."

"You t-think s-ss-oooo," Marjorie said, sniffling and trying to control herself.

"Let's wait and hear, honey."

The Russells were completely quiet now. Perhaps it had finally dawned on them. They stood there like overaged delinquents, stupid blank looks on their faces.

Marjorie thought what it would be like to be left alone for the rest of her life with no one but the Russells to turn to, and in that moment she appreciated her fine, decent parents more than she ever had before.

I will be all right, she told herself.

Steven will be all right.

* * *

After many, many days of sleepless nights and anxious mornings, the telegram finally arrived. The message was simple but devastating. Marjorie would always remember the moment. It was in mid-afternoon and she was home from the bakery. Her parents didn't want her to work until she heard definitely about Steven one way or the other, as her mind just wasn't on her job. It was a beautiful sunny day, though the weather was quite cold, and she had gone out to take a brisk, invigorating walk. She felt the warmth from the sun on her face. Combined with the bracing coolness of the frigid air around her, it was intoxicating. She felt glad to be alive. She had just convinced herself that Steven must be alive, too. There was just so much havoc over there, so much red tape, that was all—she would have heard by now if he were dead. She was feeling truly optimistic for the first time since that horrible Sunday.

Then she saw the man on the stoop, holding a telegram.

She took it, went inside, opened it, read it, collapsed. An

hour later she picked herself up off the floor and called the bakery.

Her mourning began.

* * *

Forty-seven years later and Marjorie Russell was still in mourning.

The street she lived on consisted of rather old family homes that were inhabited by other elderly or retired people like herself, or by young couples with children and pets. Once upon a time she had been on a last-name basis with half the people on the block, and a first-name basis with the rest. She knew all the children's names and they were always cute and polite to her. "Hello, Mrs. Russell," they'd say as she walked from the bus stop to her door.

Now there were a lot of new families who were very private and into themselves, and many of the old couples had died or moved to Florida. The soda shop on the corner had been replaced by a Video Heaven, and people sold drugs to school kids in the small park down the street. But it was still a nice neighborhood, she often thought, almost as nice as it had been those many years ago when she took a walk to renew her faith and optimism and came home to find her whole life shattered. There were still friendly people and adorable children.

"Hi, Marge," called out a thirtyish blond woman with bangs and chipmunk cheeks from across the street. Ethel Myerson. A lovely woman. Marjorie had sat with her children once or twice on the weekends. Ethel had a fine husband; a handsome man and a good provider. Those children were always dressed in such lovely outfits...

She passed by the Porters' house. Viola and Richard Porter. They were a nice couple in their sixties whom Marjorie had known for decades. But they had never become close with Marjorie. They'd had each other for tea now and then over the years, but nothing ever developed. Still, she knew they would do her just about any favor if she asked for it. They were good people.

Derek Hanson, the nice-looking son of the insurance agent and the realtor, was bringing out the garbage as she passed his house. "Hi," he said brightly.

She smiled and said hello. Derek got better looking every year. He was going to college in September. *He would have been good for Connie.* She wondered what *her* child would have been like, her daughter...

Don't think about that.

She walked past two more houses and was finally home.

There was a man standing on her stoop.

"Mrs. Russell? What's wrong?"

It was only Arnold, the young man from around the corner who mowed her front lawn twice a month. He was an enterprising little lad. He would always stick elegant little invoices for his services in the mail slot in her door, which, she assumed, was what he was doing now. "Going away with my folks to Cape Cod next week," he explained. "So I thought I'd mow the lawn early."

Early was right. The lawn didn't really need it, but he probably required spending money for the vacation. She opened her bag and handed him several dollars. "That's fine, Arnold. Here you go now."

"Oh, there's no hurry."

Sure. "As long as you're here, you might as well take it, Arnold, unless you want me to wait for a final notice."

"Huh? Oh...yeah. Sure. I'll take it. Thanks, Mrs. Russell."

He scooted down the path to the sidewalk and was around the corner before she could get the door open. She tore up the invoice lying on the floor under the mail slot—such a childish scrawl he had for a sixteen-year-old—and put her small bundle of groceries down on the table by the coat closet. She sighed heavily. She was weary. The boy had sure given her a start.

Why was she having all these daydreams about Steven, about her parents, the Russells, about…

Mommy, Mommy, she isn't breathing.

She couldn't hold it back anymore. She had thought about Steven often enough before the past two weeks, but never about the baby. It was just too painful. She felt such crushing guilt—she hadn't had the child long enough to love her the way she loved Steven. She felt like a monster. But how much tragedy could one person stand? She tried never to think about Connie, but all those nightmares and daydreams were bringing it back for the first time in years.

She slumped onto the sofa—not the same one she'd sat on that dreadful December 7, but almost as old—and relived it. She was just too weak to fight it anymore.

* * *

Marjorie thought she heard the baby crying.

The one good thing about Steven's death, she supposed, was that her parents didn't berate her over the fact that her child was born something less than nine months after her wedding. Everyone in the neighborhood was sympathetic, though she'd overheard one wretched woman—her mother's confidante since grade school—tell her mother in the kitchen when they thought she was outside: "She probably only got married 'cause she was pregnant. Maybe she didn't love the fellow. That way she'll get over it faster."

Marjorie loved her baby girl. Connie, she named it, after her dead aunt and godmother who'd died in a bus accident in '38. Connie was so cute and cuddly. So delightful and animated. A happy baby. Connie had her father's eyes. She was beautiful.

It was funny: Connie helped Marjorie keep her mind off her dead husband even as she reminded her of him.

She pushed aside her sheets and blankets and cooed softly, "I'm coming, baby, I'm coming."

It was three in the morning according to the clock, which she could see clearly in the moonlight coming through the window. Sometimes she was so groggy when the baby woke her that she would walk right past the crib and head down the hall, thinking she was still in that apartment she'd rented with Steven instead of back in her parents' house. She was heading for that nursery where she'd smelled the incense and seen the marks on the floor, and smelled that awful stench, smelled…

Death. She'd smelled death in that room.

Marjorie shrugged away the unpleasant thought and went over to the crib.

That's funny. She could have sworn she'd heard the baby crying, but now she was completely still and quiet.

Too quiet.

Marjorie turned on the bedroom lights. She bent over the crib, removed the blanket, and tried to see the gentle rise and fall of her baby's chest. She leaned over and tried to feel the child's breath. Nothing. She reached down and picked up Connie…

And a moment later started screaming.

* * *

The doctors didn't know what had killed her baby girl. She had died in her crib. Goblins in the night. A stench in the nursery. Death, death, death.

On the couch, worn out from her crying, Marjorie sank into slumber.

Amid the bones, the skulls, the shattered teeth and fingers, Steven was rising to his feet, looking up at her, screaming, reaching out and upward, trying to get to her, trying to tell her, warn her, trying, trying, trying…

A dark shadow fell between Steven's face and Marjorie's point of view.

The shadow smelled like the nursery and the nursery smelled like death.

Marjorie saw a hand, a claw, gnarled and bony, and in that hand was a tiny figure.

Connie was clutched in that hand.

She could see through the dark figure, see her husband still appealing to her, still screaming, trying to reach her—

Her husband tried to get through the enveloping darkness, but couldn't make it. Neither could the darkness completely overwhelm her husband. It was a stalemate.

Marjorie didn't know what to do.

And then she was awake.

Resolved, frightened, she pulled Charles Emerall's card out of her purse and started dialing.

CHAPTER THREE

Oahu, Hawaii

It was the peacocks that finally did it.

Timothy Zacharides had been having trouble getting to sleep that night. First it was a simple lack of weariness that was surprising to him, considering how hard he had been gardening that day, and how early he had gotten up in the morning; he'd been careful not to consume too much coffee, either. Finally, a vague fatigue had settled in and he was sure he was drowsy enough to succumb to Morpheus as soon as his head hit the pillow; almost immediately after, however, his inadequate digestive system acted up and he got the kind of cramps that would keep him awake the rest of the night if they were allowed to continue. He took some chewable tablets and felt a little better in about three-quarters of an hour, but by then he'd started to brood about things, to worry, and no matter how hard he tried to think of less-troubling matters, to think of *nothing*, he felt his mind and stomach boiling over again and it was just no use. He turned on the light and read some more, just a light, entertaining mystery, and when he finally felt tired again, he put away the book and shut out the light for the fourth time that evening.

But then those damnable peacocks.

They were up in the hills behind his house, wild male peafowls with four-foot plumage and excitable ways, beautiful animals who normally stayed far away from inhabited areas. He hardly ever saw them; he only heard them. At night. Previously their cries—screeches, really—had occurred only sporadically, one more nocturnal animal noise amid so many on Oahu, and they were not in the least bit disturbing. But just recently, the past few days, no more than a week or two, the birds had started a nighttime cacophony so loud and piercing that it was as if a bobcat had been loosed in their midst. Perhaps one of the island's wild boars. His neighbors were at a loss to explain it. Something was disturbing the peacocks, but he hadn't the slightest idea what it could be.

Or did he?

Well, he wasn't going to get any sleep tonight. If he were tired enough not even the peacocks would have disturbed him, but tonight an awful restlessness had taken hold of him and he knew he'd have to make up the lost sleep the next day. He got out of bed, went into the kitchen, and looked through the refrigerator for something that would satisfy his mild appetite and not upset his delicate constitution.

He knew what was upsetting the peacocks, dammit! The same thing that, according to reports, was affecting the other wildlife on the island, that was affecting some people, his pets, even Timothy himself.

It was some sort of vibration in the air, a hesitation, an expectation—*a neural anxiety, a collective apprehension*—as if Oahu itself were preparing for a disaster of epic proportions that only the island knew about, as if it were sending signals to all the inhabitants that they could perceive only on a psychic, subliminal level.

A warning, a forecasting.

An omen.

Timothy had been trying to ignore it all, trying to tell himself that he was an old man with bad nerves and a lousy stomach, and every little twitch, stomach convulsion, bit of nervous tension, or bout with insomnia did not—repeat, *did not*—mean the world was coming to an end. But he of all people knew how tenuous the fabric of nature and sanity could be, how powerless people truly were in this world they thought they owned. And his anxiety had little to do with nuclear holocaust, though the disaster he feared was easily as terrible and as mind-boggling to contemplate.

If only there were others on Oahu with whom he could consult. Wouldn't it be terrible if it were just an old man's frantic imaginings? *Wouldn't it be wonderful?*

But there were few if any people on the island who shared his peculiar interests. Some of the older natives might share his beliefs in ancient demons, but they could be such a foolish and superstitious lot that he was appalled at the prospect of conversing with them. They would meekly submit to their fate, to the power of the Old Gods as if it were preordained, as if they were deserving of oblivion for assorted, silly "sins." Of course, modern mainland Americans were scarcely better, with their churches, fundamentalists, televangelists screaming about evil and perdition...and then sleeping with the nearest hooker. He had no patience with ninnies and hypocrites. They would all blame the coming holocaust on sinning.

But people would laugh at him if he told them what he believed. They'd gleefully suggest that AIDS was a punishment from God, a punishment from a supposedly merciful deity who would kill "innocent" children along with "lustful promiscuous hedonists," but laugh if he suggested the true danger lay not in God's punishment but in the malicious advances of a strike force from another dimension that had no more sense of conscience than Huns or Vikings or plundering pirates.

But the funny thing was, even with all he'd witnessed over his eighty-two years, he had trouble believing it could actually happen. Timothy could simply not imagine his own worst scenario coming true.

Which was why he hoped the bad feelings he had had for the past couple of weeks had more to do with intestinal gas than with demonic infestations.

Are you going mad, old man? Have you finally lost your noodle?

It was nearly dawn. He pulled some bread and cheese out of the refrigerator and made himself a sandwich. He put down the knife for a moment and sighed heavily. If only he could get rid of this growing apprehension, the sense of life coming to a crossroads—or a dead end. Perhaps it wasn't concern for the world he felt, but for himself. Perhaps the tragedy he sensed on the horizon was not world disaster but simply his own approaching demise. It was long overdue, he knew.

Timothy had outlived just about everyone he had ever known and loved. Three wives, three sons, two daughters—one by one all had succumbed to accident, disease, or, incredibly, old age, even though their old man was still alive and kicking at the time. Timothy didn't know why he had remained in such good health. True, he rarely smoked or drank, stayed out of the sun—as much as it was possible to do on a tropical Hawaiian island—and tried to keep moderate hours. His mind was kept keen by an addiction to books—as well as simple luck. His diet was bland and functional, a necessity with his nervous stomach. Luckily, food had never mattered that much to him. His daily bread was a thirst for knowledge, an unquenchable desire to sate his bottomless curiosity.

Timothy had several degrees, spoke many languages, and had taught both anthropology and sociology at outstanding universities throughout the world. He had traveled extensively. Among his three wives were a well-known book author who left him for another woman, a glamorous movie actress of the thirties who had committed suicide many years after their divorce, and an ardent feminist, his last wife and greatest love, who had died of cancer some years before. His children had included a conservative Senator (the black sheep of the family), a game show host (the embarrassment of the family), a journalist (one of his pride and joys), another college professor (a genius!), and a lady astronaut who died in an accident on the freeway after hurtling through space without mishap. Truly, life's little ironies had not escaped him.

But they were all alive, his family, all alive somewhere in the void, he was convinced. They watched him and listened to him, and heard his thoughts when he talked about them to himself. Unlike the housewives who read supermarket tabloids, his beliefs were not the product of simple-minded conditioning, religious training and wish fulfillment; he believed because he had actually *spoken* to the dead.

He was sitting down at the table to eat his sandwich, slowly chewing each morsel with uncanny thoroughness, when he heard the patter of four little feet on the linoleum floor. It was Cracker, his beloved Irish Setter. Cracker was eight years old and very much her own person. He suspected the dog would hardly bother with him at all were it not for the fact that he fed her and took her for walks. She often disdained his affection, which made those rare moments when she accepted it even more precious. Her four feet planted firmly on the floor, she stood stock-still about a foot from the table—and his sandwich—and let out a petulant, frustrated whoosh of breath that indicated she expected part of that sandwich and there were no two ways about it.

So far Cracker had not been affected by whatever aura or force had affected the peacocks—if that was what it was—but the dog was normally so dense and naturally morose that it was difficult to perceive any changes in her behavior. Was she abnormally depressed, or just her usual lazy self? Silly bitch.

He would miss her when she was gone. Assuming he outlived her.

He now preferred pets to people. He had another dog, an excitable male schnauzer whose personality was in direct contrast to Cracker's; he was still asleep on his bed in the living room. There was a cat, Bernice, named after his second wife, the movie star, an ominous black Angora that he hardly ever saw except at feeding time; and in the den was a large, rather fearsome parrot with a foul mouth and evil disposition that for some reason he nevertheless found utterly charming. He loved and respected animals and occasionally feared them. Except Cracker, the pets all seemed rather tense the past few days, but perhaps they were picking it up from their owner.

He had retired to the Hawaiian Islands twenty years ago. Back then Oahu had not been as built up, or as heavily populated, as it was now. Luckily, even today the heavier concentrations of people were in Honolulu and Waikiki; in spite of the skyscrapers in some areas, there were still spots on the island where the scenic beauty and sense of isolation had not yet been perverted by loads of tourists and soaring condominiums. There were absolutely no billboards allowed on the island to mar its splendor, for which he and the other residents were eternally grateful. There was plenty of vulgarity in Honolulu and elsewhere, but the Oahu of his "youth" was still very much in evidence. Twenty years later it still took his breath away. It was a good life and he was thankful.

Until now.

It might just be old age, a complete breakdown of all systems, physical and mental, but he didn't think so. Something was wrong on Oahu. Terribly wrong. The reverberations were unmistakable. He had been involved with things of this nature before and he knew the signs. Another of life's ironies: He had moved here to forget all that, to forever turn his back on the dark side of "life," to close the door on his forbidden knowledge, but now it seemed that right here in his home he was on the verge of experiencing a psychic upheaval that made those he had lived through before seem like Sunday-school picnics by comparison.

He kept thinking: *Kanaloa.*

Kanaloa was a mysterious Hawaiian god of which little was known. He was often referred to in such a way that made it sound as if he were the Hawaiian equivalent of the Christian devil. Kanaloa was the most powerful, most feared god of all, according to island elders.

Kanaloa.

He did not believe that Kanaloa himself or itself was necessarily responsible for what was happening on Oahu. He wasn't sure he believed in Kanaloa. But he believed in beings, powerful, primordial beings, *like* Kanaloa. He knew they existed. He knew how they waited. And hungered. And he believed one of those beings was in some way responsible for the reverberations he was feeling, had been feeling now, for days.

In the absence of another word, Kanaloa would do. It would do, until he knew with what—or whom—he was dealing.

He finished his sandwich, threw a bit of cheese to the dog, which eagerly devoured it, and mentally listed *the signs:*

1. Newspaper reports of increased rapes and violent crimes in the sinister dock areas of Honolulu, an increase that was completely out of proportion to normal statistics, and definitely way, way out of bounds. Nightly stabbings, gang bangs, bloody vicious sexual assaults on both males and females. Violence that was unnecessary, often without provocation and totally out of control.
2. Increased sightings of the daytime flying bats that made their home on Oahu, bats that were reported to be attacking livestock and the occasional human

—though said reports were unsubstantiated. Rats massing in ritzy neighborhoods where they were rarely seen and weren't likely to go. Attacks on children and adults by normally docile birds and insects.

3. Thousands of Portuguese men-of-war appearing out of nowhere on the windward side of the island near Kaneohe Bay, making swimming and diving in that area all but impossible. Scientists and tourist bureaus were busy making up natural explanations, but no one could really explain why the hydrozoans were massing that way, as if they were beginning to erect a barrier around the island. It was spooky. The men-of-war had a nasty sting that was extremely unpleasant to encounter, and many foolhardy tourists had already been afflicted.

4. Attacks on tourists and residents by Hawaiian hawks and wild boars that usually left people alone if they left them alone. Only now they were flying and grunting into rural areas more populated than usual and making pests of themselves with the inhabitants.

5. The rumbling of the earth itself, centering on Diamond Head. The volcano had been extinct for millennia, and few people claimed to have felt anything at all. Therefore, Timothy wasn't sure if the rumblings were for real, were psychic in origin, or both. Perhaps only he could hear and feel them.

Nature in disarray. Nature gone awry. *Unnatural.* That was always a sign. And here on Oahu it was extreme. Something was going to happen. Not too soon, true. There was time. But how much time? And what on earth could he do to stop it when it happened? To *prevent* it from happening?

So far the "signs" were still within reason. The summer

was hotter than usual, tempers were flaring, animals were affected by heat and hunger. Men-of-war had never exactly been strangers to Hawaiian shores. Neither tourist nor resident had any reason to suspect anything supernatural was occurring. Modern-day man knew that even paradise could have serpents, and wouldn't allow a few unpleasantries to interfere with his amusements.

But Timothy knew what was going on. Just as he knew it was going to get worse. Much worse.

So he sat there in his kitchen and tried not to tremble as the day broke and the screech of the peacocks reached an unnerving, deafening crescendo, but he was certain that if something weren't done soon about the situation on Oahu, he wouldn't be the only man to be driven quite mad before the summer was over.

CHAPTER FOUR

New York City

Marjorie knew she was nervous and was showing it, but no matter how hard she tried to keep the quiver out of her limbs and voice, her own body and vocal cords would simply not obey her. *This isn't a date,* she kept telling herself. *This man is not a beau, a "gentleman caller"; he has only come here at my specific request to help me in a matter of some concern. Marjorie, this is not a date!*

But it felt like a date, it did. It felt like it—the motherly way she took his coat and hung it in the hall closet, the way she fussed about with the hors d'oeuvres and offered him a drink, the polite chit chat about the weather (sunny and not too humid); not to mention the awkward frozen smiles and the times when they both spoke at once and had to chuckle afterward. Yes, it felt like a date, and that was ridiculous, for she'd never really thought of Charles Emerall in quite that manner before. Though of course he was appealing, now that she had time to really notice it.

He didn't seem nervous. He was just as smooth and continental as ever. He asked her permission first if he could smoke

—such wonderful manners—and praised the canapés she'd made and even complimented her on the standard screwdriver that only an idiot could, well, screw up, as she told him. He had laughed appreciatively. But *he* didn't seem nervous. Not a bit.

Mostly she was nervous because she was afraid he would not believe that this was only business, that she honestly required his services, and had something serious to talk to him about. But who serves drinks and hors d'oeuvres to someone you're about to hire? she asked herself. She must be giving him the wrong impression. Still, this wasn't exactly, say, a client-lawyer or doctor-patient relationship. It seemed to Marjorie that there was no standard behavior when it came to dealing with a "private, spiritual investigator" such as Charles Emerall.

When she had finally settled down in a seat across from where he sat on the couch, he fixed her with a steady gaze and said pleasantly, "I was quite surprised to hear from you the other day. I'm sorry I couldn't drop by before tonight. But I'm very anxious to hear your story."

Marjorie's eyes watched her hand as it idly scratched at a non-existent spot on the chair arm. "Perhaps—perhaps we should come to some...arrangement...first." She took a second to swallow the phlegm that had collected in her throat. "I mean, I want to talk to you in your professional capacity, you see—at least, I *think* I might require your services. I mean, you *do* do this for a living and—"

Charles smiled. "You have invited me over for dinner. Consider that my fee for your 'initial consultation.' Once you tell me what the problem is, should you decide to engage my services, we can then discuss terms. Besides, Marjorie—I may call you Marjorie?"—she nodded—"nowadays my investigations are mostly a pastime, something for an old retired man to keep busy with. I am not looking to make a lot of money at it."

Now her hands were working at the muscles in front of her neck. "I see. Well, then, it will still be nice to talk to somebody about what's been happening to me."

"I assume it has to do with your late husband. After the incident the other afternoon—"

"Yes, yes, you're right. As I told you on the phone, the dreams I mentioned at the restaurant the other day have been getting worse. You said something about omens and warnings, and I told you it's been as if Steven were trying to contact me. But Mr. Emerall—"

"Uh-uh. Charles, please."

"Yes, Charles. Charles—I'm not sure if I even believe in a spirit world or an afterlife. To be honest, I've never understood these gullible old women who go to mediums and try to contact their late husbands' spirits and spend all kinds of money in the company of crystal balls and gypsies—" She stopped abruptly and raised one finger to her lip. "Oh, I hope I'm not offending you, Mr.—Charles. It's just that I don't know if I really think there's anything *to* this spiritualism."

"I'm not offended, Marjorie. I'm *glad* you're not one of those silly people you were describing. I've met them—and it's very easy for them to be victimized by someone unscrupulous and greedy, and I would not want that to happen to you. I must confess for a moment I was afraid—well, I can see you're too level-headed for that."

Afraid of what? Marjorie wondered. Had Charles actually thought she was some kind of dingbat, some kind of silly and lonely widow who was ripe for exploitation? If she were any judge of character she did not believe he was the type to exploit that kind of person, but it hurt a little that even for a moment he had thought she was something to be "looked after" or pitied.

"I try to be level-headed," she replied, more testily than she'd intended, "though it isn't easy in today's world. As for my dreams...well, maybe I really ought to see a psychiatrist."

She took a sip of ginger ale and wiped her lips with a dainty paper napkin that had a cheery blue-and-green pattern on it. "Maybe that's really what I ought to do."

"No, no, no," Charles insisted. "Don't let bad dreams, unusual dreams, make you think you're going crazy. That's what I'm here for, Marjorie. I want you to describe your dreams to me in every detail—leave nothing out—and perhaps I'll be able to help you interpret them. I might be able to help you determine if you're truly undergoing a psychic or supernatural experience, and if Steven is somehow trying to contact you through your dreams. If that's the case, we'll decide how best to proceed, perhaps consult a medium—and it will be a genuine medium, not a charlatan, I assure you. I've been involved in this long enough to tell a fake from a real one, that's for certain."

Marjorie shifted uneasily in her seat. "It all sounds so creepy."

"It can be creepy," he agreed. "But not if you take it on its own terms. The occult world ceases to frighten if you accept that it's simply, in its own strange way, another part of natural experience, a part that most of us are cut off from and therefore do not completely understand. For instance, if the lights were to suddenly go off in this room it might be pretty scary—especially if this were wintertime and in the dead of night—but even though the lights would be out we would still be sitting here in safe, comfortable surroundings with each other for company. And there's nothing scary about that, is there? It's the same with the occult world; it seems scary because it's unfamiliar. But if the truth were known, it may be no more frightening or dangerous than the world we walk around in every day."

Marjorie made a fluttery motion with her fingers. "Well, that's a relief. Then you don't think I'm in any danger?"

He paused almost imperceptibly before answering and Marjorie didn't like the look in his eyes. "No, of course not," he said. It didn't help matters when he added cryptically, "but I haven't heard a description of your dreams yet."

All of a sudden she felt rather foolish; she had been counting on Charles Emerall but now he was telling her that his spiritual interests were more of a hobby than a profession, just a way to keep busy. For all she knew he could be nothing more than some weirdo who went around printing up esoteric business cards just for the hell of it—and to impress lonely old widows.

"Before I get into the dreams," she said, trying, and failing to adopt a no-nonsense businesslike tone, "can you tell me more about how you…how you got interested in spiritualism? Your background? What you've done in the field?" She might find out his experience in the occult consisted of nothing more than reading a couple of books on the subject and entering the "Haunted Mansion" at an amusement park with his grand-children.

But he surprised her. Charles Emerall, it turned out, had once been a licensed private investigator (she couldn't picture him doing the Mike Hammer routine no matter how hard she tried) and had studied criminology—even lectured on the subject and taught classes—at major U.S. and European universities. He had been a consultant on various well-known cases that had stumped the police and been called in frequently in other instances to aid in an investigation in his capacity as private detective. "I am not a Sherlock Holmes," he told her very emphatically. "I was simply a determined, diligent man who believed that persistence was the corner-stone of any investigation."

His career had proceeded very well and had made him a wealthy man until tragedy struck in his mid-fifties. "My wife Clara committed suicide. The details are too depressing to go into, but I felt responsible. My investigative work took me away from her for long, long periods. And she was ill. It was about this time that I took on the strangest case of my career, just to get through my grief. I had been planning to retire just before Clara's death, to be with her more.

"It was a classic locked-room puzzle. A man in Los Angeles who professed to be a satanist had been found dead, butchered, in a meat-storage locker downtown. He had fixed the door—the only entrance and exit—in such a way that no one could get in while he enacted his rituals. The police were completely stumped. The case was never solved, has never been solved to this day. He had clearly been trying to call up some mythical demon. Anyway, it was the first case I'd ever worked on where there seemed to be *no solution*. Oh, I have not solved every case—but at least those unsolved cases did seem to have several possible explanations, even though the honestly seemed *impossible*. No one could have gotten in to kill this man, and yet the condition of the body made it clear that he had not killed himself."

Marjorie thought she knew what Charles was driving at and it was giving her the willies. Just a moment ago he had been talking about how "safe" the occult world was, had assured her that she was in no danger. Now she was beginning to think it would be safer to take a walk in Times Square after midnight than to get involved in anything of a supernatural nature.

"Are you trying to tell me some demon got him?" Marjorie said, staring her dinner guest right in the eye as if challenging him.

"No, no—I just meant that it was a case, involving spiritualism, that I could not solve, that no one could solve. It suggested that there might be...other factors at work in the world...that we don't normally take into consideration. It started my mind thinking: *Had* I come up against a genuine supernatural incident?"

He must have noticed the apprehensive look in Marjorie's eyes because he immediately added: "Don't be scared, Marjorie. Even if that man had been killed by a demon, he had been in the process of calling one up, he was actively engaged in occultism, and of a very dangerous variety, I might add. That's not the same thing as someone passively involved, such as you are, someone merely having dreams about her late husband."

There was a difference, that was true. Marjorie felt better and told him so.

"Anyway," he continued, "I later had occult experiences of my own, which cemented my curiosity about the field."

Marjorie leaned forward in her seat, especially interested in hearing what he had to say at this point. "What happened?" she asked.

He cocked his head thoughtfully and said, "Well, I started to have dreams about my late wife." He anticipated her reaction and said, "Oh, I know that sounds quite normal; it's natural to be 'haunted' by someone you had once loved and who died, in part, because of your neglect. But the *intensity* of these dreams..." He shook his head. "...the same bizarre elements over and over again."

Marjorie knew exactly what he meant.

"It was like she was calling me—I wasn't sure if she was forgiving me or tormenting me, or in trying to tell me of her forgiveness she was inadvertently tormenting me. All I know is that I was and am convinced that somehow her spirit was trying to reach me." He paused to sip some of his drink, as his throat was now sounding dry and scratchy with a vulnerable little quiver in it that spoke volumes.

Marjorie seized the moment to say, "That's what my dreams are like, all right. Did you ever find out what your wife was trying to tell you?"

"Not exactly. It isn't always clear—in fact, in most cases communications from the spirit world are never clear." He smiled tensely. "We and they are not on the same 'wavelength,' I'm afraid. I tried to contact Clara through a medium, and in part, I think, we were successful. The medium told me things only Clara could have known. But in the end I think the medium only told me what I wanted to hear—that I was not responsible for Clara's suicide, that she did not blame me. But I suspected he was as confused as I was.

"But from that experience came my obsession with the occult. I read, studied, everything I could find, consulted with experts, learned about dreams and their possible meanings. After awhile I was not just an expert in criminology, but on the spirit world, although I have virtually no psychic ability of my own. I offered my services in criminal investigations where I suspected the occult may have been, or definitely was, involved. I gained more experience from these cases, but was frustrated. The police would assume I was some kind of 'sensitive' who could divine what had happened through paranormal means. I merely wanted to offer my assistance by applying my knowledge of the occult to the criminal circumstances under scrutiny. In most instances, it was not a happy partnership. I did some good, I suppose."

Marjorie knew what it was like to lose a loved one, but her mind was so awhirl with all this new information that she said nothing about Mrs. Emerall's tragic passing. Part of her reticence to offer condolences—aside from the fact that the woman had died many years ago—was that she suspected, although Charles was clearly a good man, that his neglect of his wife *had* largely been responsible for what had happened. He was bringing out such odd conflicting feelings in her; curiosity and attraction one moment, dread and dismay the next, and not all of the "negative vibes" had to do with the occult.

"I'm so confused," she said. "You say you were contacted by your late wife in dreams, that there's no doubt in your mind"—she waited while he nodded affirmatively—"which means it's entirely possible that Steven is trying to contact me. But that presupposes so much, Charles. That there is life after death, for instance. But does that mean there's a heaven or hell? I've always believed in God, in *a* god, some form of God, at least—though I suppose people would call me an agnostic. But everything else I find so hard to accept. I want to believe —in God, in the spirit world." She paused a moment and tried to organize the rush of thoughts aching to get out of her. "But according to most religions, people...slumber...until they are, well until we *all* are, 'called' on Judgment Day. But if that's true, if no one goes to heaven or hell until Judgment Day, if they're all 'asleep,' then how can all these restless spirits be so busy contacting us, invading our dreams, watching over us...? Aren't they supposed to be at rest, in limbo, until the end of the world comes and all of us are judged before God?"

Charles smiled very broadly and nodded. Marjorie got the feeling he was pleasantly surprised to find her so stimulating. Well, she may have only worked in a butcher shop, but that didn't make her a dope.

"A very good point," he said. "There may or may not be a literal or figurative heaven and hell, a Judgment Day, a God— but that may have little to do with an afterlife in any case. May I suggest two possibilities? In a religious sense, these restless spirits, as you call them, could be in purgatory, suffering to expiate their sins before being allowed to enter heaven on Judgment Day; this may explain their desperation, their need to be in touch with us. Or we could look at purgatory in a scientific manner. Perhaps, after death, our souls or psychic energy or astral selves or whatever you want to call them, go into a different place, a different state of being, an alternate universe, the youngsters would call it, a new dimension. Perhaps this alternate dimension has a landscape that is part beautiful, part hideous, and completely unimaginable to those of us who are still alive."

He scratched his cheek slowly for a moment or two, then added: "Then there is the theory that spirits, ghosts, are people who should have 'passed on,' but who in some form— as energy, perhaps—stay on earth to haunt the living. People who have died in the prime of life, before completing an urgent task, who have committed suicide—the possibilities are endless. All I can say is I believe that in some manner life can continue after death, although not necessarily in the accepted Judeo-Christian ethic, and that there may be alternate universes out there, and sometimes these two... concepts...can fuse together." He sipped his screwdriver, then added: "Does this make any sense to you, Marjorie?"

Marjorie knew his eyes were upon her, waiting for an answer. She simply lifted her glass of ginger ale and said, "I think *I* should have had a screwdriver, too, Charles."

He broke out into a warm, infectious burst of laughter. When it subsided he said, "Marjorie, you are a delightful person. I can't tell you how wonderful it is to meet someone who neither blindly accepts nor rejects the spirit world, but simply leaves her mind open to any and all possibilities."

She smiled back at him, lifted her glass and slowly sipped the dregs of her soda and ice. Meanwhile she thought furiously: *To think! Steven might be alive somewhere, somehow —someday I might be with him again. To think! To think that Steven's mind and memory might have lived on all this time.* It was certainly a better proposition than discovering that her dreams were caused by a brain tumor or something.

Flushed with a certain quiet excitement she put her empty glass down firmly on the coffee table near the chair and whispered: "But why after all this time?"

"Pardon me?"

"Why has Steven taken so long to get in touch with me?" She sniffed. "That sounds so funny."

Charles had no real answer for that one. "Who knows? Perhaps you weren't receptive enough before. Perhaps he was afraid it would reopen old wounds. Perhaps, in this *Sheol* he is wandering in, something of great importance is about to happen; the landscape is changing."

The landscape is changing. That struck a chord in Marjorie, but she didn't know why. *Something about to happen.* The landscape, the landscape...

She remembered an odd word he'd used a moment ago. "What does '*Sheol*' mean?"

"It's the Hebrew word for the underworld," he explained.

She nodded absently. "Really?" *The landscape is changing.*

"There's something you should know," she told her guest. "Steven was very interested in the occult. At least he was before we were married."

"To what extent? Was he serious about it?"

"I was never sure. We were so young then. Practically children. It might have been just a game to him, but he seemed pretty intense about it at times. He wore this weird amulet. And he had books on casting spells and—"

She thought about the man found butchered in the meat-storage locker, calling up a demon. But that was silly...Steven was killed in the war. *It wasn't a demon, it was a bomb.*

"I'm glad you've told me this. It may be important. Can you remember anything else?"

"I haven't thought about it in years. I remember better, happier times with Steven. I was never interested in that obsession of his; it never made any sense to me. He didn't fool around with it or talk much about it after we were married. But he still wore that amulet all the time; even left it on when he came to bed."

She got to her feet and said, "Let me check the dinner. I hope you like chicken. We should be eating in just a few minutes."

She walked into the kitchen and poked about in the oven. Everything smelled delicious. For a moment her confusion and sadness faded and she just allowed the cooking smells to envelop her in the warmth and anticipation they engendered. Nothing could touch her in this kitchen when she was making a meal.

If only I were making it for Steven.

All these years later, and all other men did for her was remind her of Steven. She realized it was pathetic but didn't quite care.

That moment she decided to go ahead with her plans and to tell Charles all about her dreams, every single detail she could remember—including her dream of Connie—convinced that doing so might help in some way to reunite her with Steven. She knew it was unlikely, the ambition of a fool, but she didn't care; she only wanted to feel Steven, to feel just his energy if need be, even if it were only for one last time before letting go forever.

* * *

The dream she had that night was the absolute worst of all.

All the familiar elements came one after the other: the dark enclosure, the piles of skeletons; the dead man with the decaying flesh rising to his feet from amidst the bones; the blood seeping from the metal walls.

The element that had been introduced recently came again: the dark shadow, the gnarled hand clutching Connie; only tonight it clutched Steven, held him tight in its cruel, unrelenting grasp.

Steven's face grew closer and closer, the eyes and mouth widening, but the dark hand tried to hold him back, tried to pull him back down into the pile of skeletons. The skeletons now darted and danced about, became veritable dervishes, but it was as if they were animated from *without*, as if some outside force was making them move because their souls had long since vanished. Skeletal hands reached out to clutch at Steven's writhing form, still grasped in the enormous, clutching hand. It was as if a black awesome God had snatched him up with disdain, but in spite of that disdain Steven still kept struggling, kept fighting back, would not cease movement no matter how hard the black hand squeezed or crushed him.

Steven tried to pull out of the hand even as the skeletons tore at his body. Angry skulls bit into his arms and legs with their teeth and nibbled away small chunks of flesh. Steven could not get free of the giant hand no matter how hard he tried, so he had only one course of action remaining. He began to *pull out of his very skin*, to wrench free of his muscle and tissue, to burst out of the surrounding vessels and ligaments like a pit squeezing out through the juicy pulp of a fruit of its own volition.

The top of Steven's skull cracked and protruded through his scalp as the skeleton contained within the flesh began to *shed* that flesh, began to rip out of the confining meat in a burst of pain and spattering fluid. The pressure of the encircling hand actually worked in Steven's favor, until finally the full set of bones simply popped out from the body like so much paste from a tube.

Before the hand had tightened and foiled its plans, Steven's skeleton was racing up toward Marjorie's viewpoint until its empty eye sockets were staring right into her slumbering eyeballs. The skull's mouth opened wide and screamed.

Marjorie!

* * *

Marjorie woke up instantly. She was shivering uncontrollably and covered with a thick sheath of perspiration. Her sheets were soaked. Her body would not stop trembling. Her hand reached out to find the lamp on the night table but only succeeded in overturning it. Finally, she jumped out of bed and, screaming at the top of her lungs, hurtled down the corridor and staircase in darkness until she made her way to the kitchen. She hurriedly flipped on the light switch and collapsed into a chair at the table. There, bathed in the soft glow of the light overhead and the lingering odors of the roast chicken dinner, she sat quietly until the trembling receded and she could breathe. The high-pitched noise, the odd whine or screech that had followed her all the way down from the bathroom, receded until she finally realized with a start that it had been issuing from her own mouth. *She could still see the skull, still feel its impossible breath on her lips as if it had reached in for a phantom kiss, the grinning mouthlike orifices on each and every tooth that opened both in harmony and discord...*

Marjorie knew something had to be done.

She was finally, incontrovertibly convinced: in some way, somewhere, her husband was alive.

And he desperately needed her help.

CHAPTER FIVE

"Doesn't the water look lovely?" Charles was saying. "All the boats and the lights."

Marjorie nodded and took another sip from her water glass, wondering if this dinner engagement had really been a good idea. But here she was in Sheepshead Bay, sitting at a candle-lit table near the water, dining with a stranger who wanted to talk to her about dreams and spirits and the ghost of her late husband. All the times she'd thought of having a date with someone, she'd never thought of it happening in quite this fashion.

It seemed to Marjorie that everything had happened so fast and yet so slowly. It was only a day since Charles had dinner at her house and yet she'd known him, in a sense, for quite a while. She recalled telling Charles all about her dreams at the dinner table last night. Though she was sure he had meant well, and the conversation had been interesting, his analysis of her dreams had been a little disappointing. She didn't need him to tell her that Steven's spirit was trying to contact her, that her dead husband (who somehow yet lived) desperately needed her help, or that something very powerful was fighting Steven, trying to prevent him from reaching out to her. She could also figure out all by herself that those metal walls seeping blood in her nightmare were actually the chambers of the bombed sunken battleship, the U.S.S. *Arizona,* and that the skeletons represented the other dead men who had been entombed with her husband. She even knew that Connie had showed up in one dream and one dream only simply because she had been thinking vividly about her baby girl that same afternoon. Like Charles, she sensed that Connie had nothing to do with this; that her child's soul had passed on to some other plane of existence, that Connie, at least, was at peace.

No, Charles had not really shed any new light on her nightmares, but she had been impressed with his compassion and concern. He had gone through something similar with his wife. But he did say something that disturbed her:

"I have a feeling that Steven is trying to reach you for reasons that are far more important than simply to deliver a personal message. Time may pass differently in the spirit world, but it *has* been a while since he died. The dark figure in whose hand Steven is crushed suggests another, more powerful and sinister presence. Perhaps someone—even someone who is living—who represents a danger to you. But don't be frightened by any of this, my dear. Be grateful that Steven is warning you and that you have been alerted to the danger."

But she didn't like the idea of "danger." She thought of mangled corpses in meat storage lockers, of vast demonic forces beyond her ken or ability to fight, things that made everyday muggers and drug dealers seem like children by comparison.

Then that night after Charles had left she'd had that incredibly intense nightmare with Steven literally tearing out of his own flesh. Although nothing definite had been decided at the dinner table—she'd simply told Charles that she'd be in touch—that new development had made up her mind for her.

She called Charles in the morning and told him she definitely wanted him to help her if he could, even if it meant steering her to a genuine medium. She wanted him to tell her how to stop the nightmares—and how to help Steven.

So the very next evening Charles had picked her up to take her out to dinner. In the taxi he told her that he had decided to take on her "case," but only if she would proffer payment in the form of home-cooked meals and the occasional date with him, for which he would pay. She protested strenuously—but secretly was pleased and charmed by his behavior. It also convinced her that he was not a kook or a con man out to fleece widows of their savings.

He picked the restaurant in Sheepshead Bay. They were sitting at a large picture window where they could look out at the boardwalk and wharves, the fishing boats hauling in booty by the net. A brisk, not unpleasant, fishy fragrance filled the air; inside the room the aroma of cooked lobster and shrimp was tantalizing to the appetite. The table had a square red tablecloth and was set with goblets of ice water and pretty patterned china plates. After ordering two screwdrivers, they got down to business. Marjorie told him about the last dream.

He shook his head soberly and looked very concerned. "It's clear that it's getting worse. If it keeps up, it could have a terrible effect on you. Something has got to be done, Marjorie."

"That's just it, Charles. That's why I called you again. I don't know what to do. What can I do? I'm ready to try everything short of an exorcism."

He dismissed the idea with a wave. "That won't be necessary. You're not possessed. Haunted might be a better word. Haunted from afar. Someone from your past is simply trying to communicate something to you; no more, no less."

"But it's more than that, we agreed," she reminded him. "Steven needs my help. He's crying out for me. What do I do about it? How can I help someone who's been dead for nearly fifty years?"

The waitress brought their drinks. She had overheard Marjorie's last remark but tried to pretend she hadn't. They waited until she was gone before they resumed.

"Should I attend a seance?" she asked him. "Try to speak to Steven?"

"It's one possibility. But it could be a waste of time. Even if the medium contacts Steven's spirit, there's no guarantee you'll learn anything more. Mediums are limited. Even when they enter trance state and the ghost of someone dead talks through them, their words and messages are garbled and incomplete. You *might* have it substantiated that Steven is calling to you and wants you to come to him." His eyes narrowed. "You *did* get that sense—that he wanted you to physically go to some other place to help him?"

"Yes."

He revolved his glass in his hands and shrugged. "It's just that nothing you've told me about your dream would necessarily indicate that. He's trying to reach you, yes, but—"

"That's just it," Marjorie said. "He can't reach me. Not physically, not mentally. That dark enormous figure won't let him. I can't explain it—it's as if I *have* to go to *him*. It's a feeling I wake up with every morning. A feeling that I have to travel nearer to him, that he can't tell me what's wrong until I'm closer..."

Charles nibbled on a piece of bread. "Maybe he wants you to find something. Or wants to remove you from danger. Perhaps he knows of some coming tragedy." He waited until his mouth was empty and said, "I once knew of a woman who dreamt that her late husband kept telling her to move out of the house. Each night the dream got worse and more intense. Finally she gave up and moved into her sister's apartment temporarily. That very night a plane crashed on the house where she lived; it was almost certain that she would have been killed."

That was all she needed, Marjorie thought. More anxiety. Now she'd lay awake at night waiting for the roof to cave in. "I have trouble with stuff like that," she said, a bit irritably. "How can spirits know something like that is going to happen? I don't believe in fate—at least I don't want to. To think all of history has already been written and your future is preordained, unchangeable..."

"Ah, but the dead man did change his wife's fate, didn't he?"

"I suppose so. Still, I don't understand stuff like that, what do you call it...?"

"Precognition. Some people believe that individuals with precognitive ability are simply high-level psychics who can read other people's thoughts and make conjectures on what will happen based on these subconscious messages. That's why these people are wrong as often as they're right. Their guesses can be way off the mark."

The drink was already going to her head and she wasn't in the mood for listening to more talk about precognition and sensitives and the like. She was getting impatient and wanted to know what to do about Steven. "Charles, what are you going to do to help me?"

"I'm going to order you another drink when you've finished that one. It will help you relax. You're too tense."

"Can you blame me? Seriously. What are you going to do? I know your services are inexpensive, but that doesn't mean I won't expect results." She gave him a smile just to show that she was, partially, teasing.

Charles leaned back in his chair and crossed his arms. "Well, if you really want to know what I think, I'll tell you. I think you should do as Steven has been so urgently requesting and fly to Pearl Harbor."

For a second she just sat back in her chair and looked at him. "What did you say?"

"You heard me."

"Fly to Pearl Harbor?"

"Not to be indelicate, but as you told me, his body was not one of those that was recovered. Which means that his remains are still entombed on that ship."

Marjorie wasn't sure she liked the direction this conversation was taking. "What difference does that make? Aren't we talking about his *soul* now? The soul in the *Sheol* or whatever you want to call it." She really was a little tipsy now; she supposed she'd drunk the rather strong screwdriver too quickly. "If he can show up in my nightmares, why do I have to go to where he's buried?"

A stab of sudden sadness ran through her and she had to stifle a sob. "That's *not* Steven down there in that ship. That's not Steven. Steven is some place else, some beautiful place, that's what you told me..." And then she did utter a tiny cry and put one hand over the side of her face as if to press the threatening tears back under her eyelids. "The skeletons, the blood on the walls—that's just symbolic, isn't it? He's not really there, still down there! How could he be?"

Charles placed his hand over the one Marjorie still had on the table and squeezed it, then waited a moment until she was more composed. "Marjorie, Marjorie, I'm sorry. You second-guessed me on everything else when we discussed your dreams last night—so I assumed you realized..."

She pulled away her hand and got a handkerchief out of her purse. She patted at her eyes and nose with the linen and then waited for him to continue.

"Dreams involving the dead *can* be very symbolic. But there's something about this dream, your dream, that is different. The fact that you keep seeing Steven in the very place where he died over and over again is significant. So is the fact that something is holding him back, pulling him back down with the others, who are skeletal, while Steven is still whole. Spirits can remain bound to the place where they died, particularly if they died violently and without warning, as Steven did. The ship isn't just Steven's tomb—as I said it's the very spot where he lost his life and that alone has a lot of meaning."

She interrupted: "But why not the others? There are nearly a thousand bodies on that ship that were never recovered."

Charles unfolded his arms and put his hands on the *edge* of the table. "That's what we have to go to Pearl Harbor to find out. It may be that the other souls are also trapped, but since they aren't trying to reach you, they only appear to you as skeletons. Or it may be that only Steven's soul has been bound to the ship. There may be a hundred different explanations when you're dealing with the occult."

Marjorie leaned forward anxiously. "But if that's the case—how can he reach me at all, even in my dreams?"

Charles' hand went up in a gesture of frustration. "I can't give you all the answers, Marjorie. I guess Steven's soul has enough power, for lack of a better word, to communicate with you on the subconscious, psychic level, while you sleep—but that's all. That dark presence is holding him back. But if you were actually in the vicinity of where his spirit is still bound to the earth, he might be able to reach you. If you were to just go to sleep somewhere near Pearl Harbor, undoubtedly you would at least find out what Steven is trying to tell you. There'd be no need to actually enter the ship, even if that were possible."

This was all very upsetting. It hadn't occurred to Marjorie that Steven might have been suffering all this time. "But if what you say is true—what has it been like for Steven all these years? Being trapped down there, being—"

"Marjorie, Marjorie! It isn't the same as if he were a living person. There is no hunger, no fear, no human needs. Time has probably passed very quickly for him, the wink of an eye. He might not have suffered at all."

He could say that, but Marjorie didn't believe him. She had a sense of the kind of awful loneliness her husband must have endured, loneliness and fear and probably abject horror. She desperately hoped Charles was entirely wrong about everything. She couldn't bear to think that he might be right.

Charles continued: "He may not have been aware he was even dead until recently; he may have wandered around peacefully on some psychic level, in a 'fog' we can't possibly comprehend, until he realized he should have moved on but hadn't."

"Do you think that's what he wants, for me to help him 'move on?' "

"Perhaps."

"But how can I do that? I haven't the slightest—"

"Marjorie, that's what I'm here for. We won't know how to proceed until we find out once and for all exactly what Steven wants. I cannot recommend any action or get in touch with anyone who might help us until I know what we are dealing with. As I said, I haven't all the answers. Just trust me, please."

The waitress came to take their dinner orders. Marjorie didn't feel very hungry. She was so confused. Steven was dead. Steven was alive. Steven was wandering about in the ether. Steven was trapped on a ship full of corpses. Could she reach him? Could she help him? But if she could—would she want to help him "pass on," send him away, if it meant she would no longer be able to touch him, feel him, speak to him in any way whatsoever? She just didn't know what to do. And was any of what Charles was saying true?

Yet the dreams were true; there was no mistaking that. The feelings were real. Steven—or what passed for Steven these days—was trying to reach her; he did need her help, that was clear. If there was anything she could do—she had to do it...

She had to do it no matter what the cost.

* * *

Southwestern Oahu

Keno Amahami's pick up truck blew up a storm of dust as it tore along the narrow dirt road heading down into the valley where his farm was located. He had spent all night up in the Waianae Mountains after being chased out of the house by his wife, a hot-tempered Filipino bitch he would regret marrying till the day he died. He had to get away from her fits of screaming, her carrying on, her crazy accusations. He would jump into his truck, and head out of this dry lusterless section of the island and up into the more verdant mountains to drink his brains out. Walking along one of the forgotten trails he had explored as a boy he would finally come upon a swift running *auwai* upon whose banks he would settle; he might dip his feet into the water or merely rest on some fronds until he was calmer. Then he would drink until his bottle was empty.

Keno had been born on Oahu and his wife had been his childhood *ipo.* But the hag was a sweetheart no longer, just a nasty-tempered, grizzle-faced old witch of fifty who was determined to make the sixty-year-old Keno's final years as miserable as possible.

For many years, the two of them had run one of the area's less prosperous chicken farms. It was a study in dilapidation, with a cracked, peeling house, a barn that looked as if a mild breeze might blow it over, and an ancient unused automobile rusting in the front yard that seemed to have taken root in the soil. There were a dozen chicken coops out behind the house, and the smell during the hottest months was simply ferocious. The chickens set up a cacophony that Keno was sure was partially responsible for his wife's nasty, addled brain—but the real noise came not from the hens but the roosters.

The roosters, bred for *haha moa*, cock-fighting, a popular sport in this part of Oahu, were possibly the most hideous-looking creatures of their breed. Their beaks and talons were long and sharp, and they strutted about in their pens, snapping and crowing, making such a commotion it nearly drove you crazy, as if they had nothing but contempt for the world, their masters, and each other. They were like something that had been vomited up from Hades. But Keno was proud of them, and when he sold them they brought a good price. He had two who were not for sale, though, two wicked rooster warriors who had won every fight they'd been in but would surely not last beyond one or two more.

When his wife got mad at Keno she would threaten to kill the roosters.

If she ever did that, he swore he would kill *her*.

His foot pressed down on the brake. He had to get home, *had to get home*. Just in case. Just in case she had actually done it last night. His poor roosters!

Last night he had slept under the cool leaves of the mountain trees and dreamt of roosters with female heads, with faces like his wife, women with chicken feet as well as crow's feet, pecking at him and pecking at him until he was raw and bloody, pecking until he was all blood and bones and no flesh.

He had woken up with a start when the moon was full to find that something *was* pecking at him.

It was an *io*, a Hawaiian hawk, flying in low to repeatedly stab at him with its very sharp, hooked bill and claws. The hawk was incredibly fast, streaking down out of the night sky, striking, then hurtling upward again only to start the vicious process all over.

The hawk seemed a bit hesitant when Keno fully awoke and jumped to his feet, cursing and bleeding. *What the hell!* Since when did hawks attack humans, sleeping or otherwise. He had heard that a hawk had badly injured, practically slaughtered, a small island boy the day before yesterday, but he had been just a foolish little *keiki* who may have come too close to the hawk's nest or something. But now a grown man? —impossible!

The hawk hadn't stopped its attack until he bent down, picked up a few stones, and managed a direct hit with the very first rock, following it with a barrage of smaller rocks and pebbles. The hawk had finally flown away. Even drunk, Keno was more than a match for the bird.

Pupule. Crazy.

He had taken a quick stock of his minor, but painful, injuries, mostly on the forehead where the bird had nipped as he lay dreaming, then fallen back into a stupor on the ground.

An hour later something even stranger happened.

He woke up and heard a small giggling or rasping sound, a patter of tiny feet on the trail that led to the other side of the *auwai*, tiny yips and yelps, breathing noises. Then he saw them, busy as bees, working their mischief behind the confining bushes across the stream. *Menehune!*—the Hawaiian pixies who, like the leprechauns of Irish legend, worked overnight to build, in their case, temples and ponds and other enchanted places.

Keno rubbed his eyes. He had to be seeing things. Menehune, *my God!*

The *menehune* danced about, frolicked, tittered, tore small plants out by the roots, pranced and preened, patted and shoved each other, and had themselves an altogether delightful time; it looked much more like play than work. What were they building? he wondered. But the *menehune* looked less mischievous and more demonic than he would have expected; their countenances had something about the eyes that reminded him of...

That reminded him of his roosters.

Keno shivered. They were such *ugly* little things.

Then just as he was wondering if he had completely taken

leave of his senses, the *menehune* vanished right before his eyes.

Good, he thought. They were scaring him.

He went back to sleep and woke up fairly refreshed in the mid-morning. He drank so frequently he rarely got hangovers. He swallowed the remaining few drops of liquor in the bottle, and carried it back with him along the *ala* to where he had parked his truck.

Now as he sped through the majestic sunlit valley, he passed by friends of his who lived on a flower plantation not far from his chicken farm. They stood among rows of cream, orange and brilliant crimson plumerias and waved to him enthusiastically. Keno didn't stop to chat or even wave back, though. He had to get home to his roosters. If his wife had hurt them...

He could see her in her flapping muumuu, *marching out to the pen with gun in hand, aiming and firing, aiming and firing...*

Or getting a hatchet, the kind she used to butcher the chickens, and opening the gate to the rooster pen, striding malevolently into the enclosure to hew and hack at all of his defenseless roosters.

Of course, his roosters would not die without a struggle, no siree, especially not his two favorites. They would fight her to the death. They would peck at the bitch, scratch her, claw her, fly at her in a rage. They wouldn't take her cowardly attack lying down.

But in the end he knew she'd win. Simple. She was that ornery.

He had by now convinced himself that the *menehune* he had seen had been a product of his imagination, but the injuries on his face told him that the hawk attack had been no nightmare—unless he had thrashed about in his sleep and hurt himself against a branch or bramble without realizing it. He couldn't really remember and didn't care to. In the light of day it seemed unimportant.

Hawk attacks. *Menehune.* Everything was crazy. And he knew who to blame. It wasn't drink, it wasn't his wife, it wasn't his roosters. It was the *haoles*, the white men who came to the island and wanted to turn it into a rich man's playground, the *malihinis* who had invaded his home and turned the other parts of the island into vulgar displays of avarice and commerce. Sometimes the rich bastards would drive by in their rented cars and buses and he would spit violently at the ground if he couldn't spit at them. They lived like kings while they despoiled the island, while they prompted nature to turn against even the *kamaainas*, those who had been born on the island and stayed loyal to it. Someday, someday…they would all get even. *That* was what was important.

He turned into the short road that led to the front yard of his farm. Where was the woman? *His roosters, his roosters, he had to see to his roosters…*

There was a great commotion coming from their wire and wood stake pen, though he could not immediately determine the cause of it. His wife was nowhere in sight. He called out her name, a formless dread entering his heart…

He walked over to the rooster pen. The roosters were all gathered in one side of the pen, over near the gate. They were pecking at something, *attacking* something…

He saw wet slivers of a reddish brown meat in their beaks.

Then he looked down at their feet and saw the large lump in the colorful *muumuu* laying on the ground, all covered with blood, claws, and feathers. Bile rose in his throat and his breath came in sharp, painful spurts. He sank down to his knees, sickened.

She actually tried to do it, he told himself, not sure whether to give into his understandable rage or the surprising sense of grief he felt. She actually went in there and tried to… He saw the hatchet lying near her bloodied outstretched hand, the spattered rooster blood from the few blows she'd managed to deliver before…

He had expected the birds to fight back, with their claws, their beaks; he'd expected them to fly at her in a frenzy, to fight as they had been bred and trained to fight...

But this? *This?*

The large white lump inside the tattered muumuu looked like a raw boiled crustacean ripped out of its carapace; it had no features, no eyes, no skin. The roosters continued to peck and gnaw and gobble up the strips of meat even as Keno beat furiously, helplessly, at the gate of their pen.

Keno had not expected the roosters to kill her.

He had not expected his roosters to *eat her flesh.*

CHAPTER SIX

Are you sure you've made the right decision?

This was the question Marjorie had been asking herself a hundred times during the past few hours. Now, lying in her bed at home unable to sleep, she tossed and turned and tried to block out all thoughts of what was happening tomorrow. She felt a tension and sense of indecision that was nearly unbearable. What to do? *What to do?*

Flying to Honolulu with Charles Emerall! Marjorie, are you sure it's the right thing to do? Can you trust him? Is this some mad impulse, some foolish elderly woman's final fling, a fantastic, pathetic pipe dream?

Or *was* it the right thing to do?

She had to admit: ever since she had made the decision to go to Pearl Harbor where her husband was buried, her dreams had become much less intense than before. It was as if now that Steven knew she was coming to Oahu there was no need for him to expend so much painful energy trying to get in touch with her, to convince her to come to his graveside. And she sensed somehow that *that* was exactly what he wanted her to do.

She hadn't made up her mind to go that night at the

restaurant in Sheepshead Bay. She'd had too much to think about. Over a delectable seafood dinner Charles had spoken more about his occult experiences, about his beliefs, and at least he'd slowly managed to convince her that what she was undergoing was truly of a psychic or supernatural origin. Frequently he'd touch her hand, stare into her eyes, make her feel young and attractive, as if she were somebody one could feel affection for, desire for, not just pity. It was so bizarre—Charles seemed to be courting her even as he was trying to convince her to get in touch with her late husband. Didn't he know he was at cross-purposes? Or was it all a game to him?

Two days passed after that night without communication from Charles. Neither did she get in touch with him. She was grateful for the respite. That night she had sensed his romantic overtures, despite his assurances that, should he accompany her on the trip, it would be strictly a business arrangement. A business arrangement? When she was "paying" him by letting him take her out to dinner? She didn't want to become too indebted to the man. Oh, this was ridiculous! She was too old for this. Too old for anything. But if that were the case, what on earth was she afraid of?

It had been so long since she'd been out with a man, longer since she'd slept with one. She wasn't sure if the feelings Charles had rekindled in her were because she found him attractive, was stimulated by *his* interest, or simply had a need for physical contact with *someone*—or simply because she was thinking about Steven so much lately. Young, handsome Steven. Even if Steven were shriveled and old like she was she'd want him to hold her and touch her, make love to her. It was less physical than emotional, this need for closeness, for communion. She tried to picture what he would have looked like today had he lived, but she couldn't. In her mind's eye he was eternally twenty-one.

On the third day she got a call from Charles. Dinner. Just

to talk. "We won't have to discuss Steven, Pearl Harbor, or nightmares tonight if you don't want to."

She blurted it out before she could stop herself. "You mean, this is a real date?"

"A real, honest-to-goodness date, yes."

"All right," she said.

That dinner (at a Japanese place where they discussed favorite authors and musicians) was followed by another home-cooked meal that she prepared for him over the weekend. Then dining and dancing two nights later. The two of them got along like old friends—there seemed to be no awkwardness at all, even during their companionable silences. It was all very peculiar but she didn't wonder or question; she just accepted. She couldn't have Steven—yet—but here was a real flesh and blood man who clearly liked her company and who even seemed to find her attractive. It was odd that he had come along just at this moment. He was easy to make conversation with—he liked so many of the things that she liked, including music and poetry—and he had such fascinating stories to tell about his work as a private eye. She had never met anyone like him. Who would have guessed what kind of person was hidden behind the courtly facade of the gentleman who'd come into the butcher shop? Who would have known he'd find her as interesting as she found him? He liked her simple taste in clothes, loved her cooking, didn't care that she'd led a rather sheltered existence—she was still easy to talk to and was better read than some women her age. In fact he said he envied the quiet peacefulness of her life, said he'd missed so much by running around like a maniac all the time.

She wondered if she was just a stand-in for his wife.

One night he broached The Subject again. Hawaii. Pearl Harbor. Steven. Yes, she was still having the dream, though it was not as intense as before, as if Steven sensed she was weakening, about to give in and say yes to Charles' crazy suggestion. Or could it be that the dark figure clutching Steven was growing stronger? Or perhaps Steven sensed her growing fondness for Charles Emerall and was jealous and felt abandoned? No, she would never abandon Steven. Never love anyone but him.

She was still saying that when she invited Charles in for a nightcap, still saying it when he put his arms around her and kissed her, still saying it when she started crying because this wonderful thing seemed to be happening so late in her life, and thought: if only she'd met someone like this years before, her whole life might have been different.

No, no, she had to be loyal to Steven, she thought. Then: *Steven would understand.* She was saying both things over and over again as Charles kissed away her tears, kissed her hand, bent down to place his lips and tongue on her shoulder. She wanted him beside her, wanted him to hold her, and was surprised to realize that she wanted him to make love to her, too. It was she who led him up to her bedroom. She who began undressing. In the back of her mind she saw herself and Charles as two old people fumbling in the dark, saw them through the eyes of the young and the innocent and was pained by the grotesqueness of the vision. But in her heart she saw something entirely different; something that was right, was warm, was loving. Something that mattered and was necessary. Something that was good.

The sex was not the burning, grasping, passionate kind of magazines and movies. Rather it was quiet and loving and soft, a lot of close, affectionate cuddling and kissing. Charles made a noble attempt and nearly succeeded; she felt him inside her for a moment or two, both liking and hating the solid, sharp maleness, but a moment later he was through, apologizing, and she hushed him with a kiss. That didn't matter, she told him. What mattered was that he was there and in his own sweet way had made her feel once more like a young woman, like a person who was needed and cared for.

They were not in love, no, but for just a moment they'd eased the barren feeling, the loneliness, and made human contact in a time and at an age when it was at a premium. The value of the experience was inestimable to Marjorie, and she hoped—and feared—that Charles was aware of that.

"Come with me to Pearl Harbor," she said. "I need you."

She wondered if he was disappointed now that she'd asked him, now that she'd made a firm decision to go. Perhaps now he would want her to forget all about Steven, his only possible rival.

But she was getting away with herself. They'd only known each other barely two weeks after all. But at their age, she reminded herself, two weeks was not an inconsiderable period.

"I'm glad you need me," he told her.

She felt guilty. She needed him only because of Steven. And especially because if she could not reach Steven, she would need someone to help her get over her grief and disappointment. It wasn't fair to Charles, but she had no other choice.

"Are you sure about this?" he asked her.

"I've got to do it. I've got to get to the bottom of this. For Steven's sake, I've got to. I've always meant to visit the memorial at Pearl Harbor. I feel ashamed I've never gone before but I was afraid the memories... I've got vacation time coming. Money saved up. Maybe it *is* the thing to do..."

He squeezed her hand. "I think it is. I'm sure it is."

But she wondered: did he truly realize and accept that she was doing this for Steven? That this was not to be a mere pleasure trip, a chance for them to get to know each other better, but a rescue mission to save the only man she would ever really be in love with?

She squeezed this fine man's hand back, lifted it to her lips and kissed it, and wondered about the things people did in the name of love.

* * *

And now, a few days later, the arrangements had all been made. Charles had taken care of everything. It turned out he had been to Oahu several times before and for the past few months had been planning to visit an elderly associate of his who lived there, a man he'd become friends with when they taught at the same university. He had contacted this friend, Dr. Timothy Zacharides, and told him a bit about Marjorie. Zacharides responded by inviting both Charles and Marjorie to stay in his home, which was located not far from Pearl Harbor. Marjorie let Melvin at the butcher shop know she'd be gone for two weeks and started packing immediately.

She was excited. Even if the trip was a bust on an occult basis, it was still something to look forward to. She had a million apprehensions—flying in a *plane* for several hours not being the least of them—but she knew she had to go through with it. She was carried along on a mad rush of sudden passion for life, for living, as if it were a last chance to find excitement and adventure, to make up for the drabness of her years. So caught up in this feeling was she that she did not really question what she was about to do, or consider how little she still knew about Charles (though in the past few days she'd learned a lot about him), or how much she was skeptical of the paranormal. She didn't stop to think about anything but *going.*

So this final night, before the flight from New York to Honolulu, she lay in bed and repeatedly asked herself if she was doing the right thing. It was a fine time to be asking that question, she thought, but she had to know the answer. She fell asleep with the question still on her lips.

That night she dreamed again. Steven was still there, still imprisoned, still calling for her. But as before there was a kind of relief, a lessening of torment in his voice. *He knew she was coming to help him.*

In the morning as she waited for Charles to pick her up in a taxi, she knew: she had made the right decision.

* * *

Oahu

After an uneventful but nearly five-hour flight from their stopover, Los Angeles, Marjorie was happy to set down on the runway of Honolulu International Airport. She was a little disappointed that most cruise ships no longer docked at the harbor so that she could have arrived by boat and been greeted by the traditional, stereotypical crowd of friendly lei-flinging islanders, but she was nevertheless happy she had made the decision to come. The view from the air as they approached Oahu was breathtaking and her heart beat faster at the thought of walking amidst such splendid primitive beauty.

Now of course she was surrounded by all the crass signs of so-called civilization: glass and chrome terminals, modern DC-10s, loads of jet-lagged tourists with their baggy eyes and baggages, high skyscrapers reaching up into the blue horizon from the heavily populated city of Honolulu not far in the distance. But she knew the real Oahu was hidden just behind these terminals, those buildings, and that was what really mattered. She was so dizzy with the excitement of being there that her fatigue melted away and she almost forgot the somewhat sinister purpose she had in coming to the island. Deep down, however, part of her excitement was that she was so close to Steven. *And underneath the excitement was a vague sensation of uneasiness and sorrow.*

Charles had been here before so he guided her in the right direction, down the proper hallways, got her through the bustling enormity of the main terminal with relative ease. She was sure she herself would have gotten lost. He was heading toward a restaurant inside the terminal where Timothy Zacharides would be waiting for them. Luckily their flight had been on time. As they had agreed to travel lightly—all Marjorie would really need on the island was a *muumuu* and a toothbrush—Charles was able to carry both of their small carry-on bags without discomfort.

They spotted Timothy right away when they reached the restaurant. The two men greeted each other warmly. Then Charles introduced Marjorie to the elderly anthropologist. She liked him immediately, though she was somewhat alarmed at his obvious frailness.

Timothy Zacharides looked about twenty years younger than his eighty-two years, she felt strength in his fingers when he shook her hand—but he was frightfully pale and thin, almost cadaverous. Although he really did not look much older than Charles, neither did the man look healthy. The eyes, in particular, were grim and haunted—*like my eyes*, Marjorie thought—untouched by the muscles his face brought into play when he beamed a greeting. Marjorie knew something was wrong in this man's life.

Zacharides was a tall man—about six feet—and had bright, large, twinkling brown eyes. There was a shock of tousled brown hair on his head that needed cutting, and he wore a light blue shirt, white shorts—such chicken legs! she observed—and comfortable-looking sandals. His features were even, almost handsome, and he had a wonderful smile that revealed rows of strong gleaming teeth that may or may not have been his own. A nice man, she thought.

"Welcome. Welcome to Oahu, 'the gathering place,' " Timothy said, smiling at Marjorie. He also had a slight European accent and a smooth cultured way of speaking that reminded her of James Mason or Ronald Colman.

Charles winked at Marjorie. "You'll have to forgive Tim. He has a tendency to be a bit pedantic."

Timothy laughed good-naturedly. "You'll learn all there is

to know about this island before you've left here," he assured her.

She already knew how the two men had met and become friends, and how much Charles admired and cared for his older friend and associate. She knew a bit of Zacharides' life history—his many marriages, deceased children, occult interests—but nothing that would really explain why Charles thought the man could be of service to them in regard to her dreams about Steven. On the plane Charles had explained that Timothy could be of much more use to them than just acting as host while they were on the island. "If anything," Charles said, "Tim knows more about the occult than I do. And has had many more experiences." But he wouldn't elaborate. Perhaps because he didn't want to scare her any more than he already had.

Marjorie couldn't help but notice that Timothy had a large bandage on his left hand and asked if he had hurt himself. "It's nothing," he told her. "My parrot gave me a nip this morning."

Charles scowled. "That's a big bandage. What did she do? —try to bite off your finger?"

Timothy tried to dismiss it. "Don't worry, it's nothing."

In spite of his attempt to downplay the incident with the bird it was obvious to Marjorie that he was more upset by it than he let on. Well, maybe his hand really bothered him; a bite like that could be quite painful.

As they headed out of the terminal toward his automobile —a sensible blue convertible—he said something interesting. "This will sound funny, Marjorie, but I have to ask you not to go too near my pets while you're in my house."

She shrugged compliantly. "I won't if you don't want me to."

Charles's eyebrows rose in surprise. "Why not, Tim? She'll love your animals. And they'll love her."

Timothy frowned. "They've, uh, been a bit testy lately.

Don't know what it is. Perhaps the weather. I wouldn't want Marjorie or you getting scratched or bitten."

Before Charles could pursue the matter further, Timothy changed the subject and regaled Marjorie with some statistics about the island's climate, population and must-see sights that he would be only too happy to show her during her visit. He *was* almost pedantic, and bubbly, like a tour guide, but Marjorie found it fascinating. She got a history lesson and introduction to island life all in one.

For instance, she learned that Oahu was the third-largest of eight Hawaiian Islands, and that it consisted largely of two parallel mountain ranges, the Koolau and Waianae, which were separated by vast fields of pineapple and many plantations. The island's population was 26% Caucasian, 27% Japanese; the rest was divided between Chinese, Filipino, Black, mixed, partial, and unmixed Hawaiian, and other races. You never said "north" or "south" on Oahu, but *makai* (toward the sea) and *mauka* (toward the mountains). "I'll have you speaking the language in no time," Timothy promised Marjorie.

The drive to where Timothy lived didn't take much longer than twenty minutes. He explained that the concentration of highrises in the island was mostly in the opposite direction, in Waikiki Beach, in Honolulu (with its population of over 300,000), and in the salt lake district near Pearl Harbor. "I don't live far from Pearl Harbor, by the way," Timothy said as they drove along scenic Route 78, which passed through districts that were more rural than what Marjorie had seen so far. "Charles told me on the phone that you're particularly interested in going there, but didn't say why. Just like him to be mysterious. Especially at long distance, eh, Charles? I'm anxious to hear what's up."

Marjorie was grateful when Charles replied: "Wait until we get to the house and we can all have a drink and discuss it. Speaking of being mysterious, you said on the phone that you were glad I was coming because there was something that you had to talk to *me* about that also has to do with the occult. What about it, hmmm?"

Timothy gave Marjorie a wink. "Like you said, Charles, wait till we get home."

Timothy lived in one of several housing developments located in the hills of Aiea in the shadow of the Koolau mountain range. They passed by the Pearlridge shopping center, which seemed not much different than anything Marjorie might see on the mainland, except for the palm trees, a more colorful variety of flowers, and multi-racial shoppers in light-weight casual clothing and *muumuus*. "I've got to get a *muumuu*," Marjorie said.

"We'll go shopping later," Charles assured her.

As they climbed up into the hills they drove along a narrow road which was bordered by clumps of the ever present hibiscus shrubs in nearly every hue of the rainbow, with red the dominant color. A forest of hau and milo trees, which Timothy said provided wood for canoes and other things, briefly enclosed them until they were in a smaller, more isolated development almost at the base of the mountain. The houses were spaced some distance apart but were within view of one another. They pulled up in front of Timothy's house, which was of moderate size, split level, mostly Oriental in design, and pale green and gray in color. Marjorie thought it was exquisite.

When she got out of the car the first thing Marjorie noticed was the wonderful smell, a spicy, floral aroma that Timothy assured her was noticeable all over the island. The mountains behind the house were rugged and green, laced with winding trails, and she thought she could spot the ruins of an ancient temple up near the top of one slope. Timothy led them over to a flight of steps set into the ground at one side of the house and took them down to a pair of sliding glass doors that opened into the den. Immediately outside these doors was the *lanai*, a typical Hawaiian pavilion or outdoor living room which was surrounded by flower beds, roped in by bougainvillaea and other leafy, colorful vines, and covered with a thatchy circular roof. There were several bauhinia trees in the garden sporting lovely flowers like pink orchids, and a large Australian brassaia, a rubber plant known as an umbrella or octopus plant, stood in a pot at the far end of the garden. Two tall coconut palms completed the ensemble. Timothy had worked hard on his back yard and it showed.

After accepting Marjorie's admiring compliments, Timothy opened the door to the den. A mangy-looking Irish Setter loped out beside her master's spindly legs and started past Charles and Marjorie. Marjorie, charmed, reached out her hand to pet the animal, but was warned away just in time by the low, sinister growl the dog was emitting.

"What the hell has happened to Cracker?" Charles said, as he watched the dog head for one corner of the garden where she plopped into a puddle of fur and ire, glaring at them with startling malignance. "She was never the friendliest animal, true, but she's never tried to nip anyone either, has she?"

Timothy entered the den and sighed as if relieving himself of a great burden. He pointed to where Charles could momentarily rest the baggage. "All of my animals, as well as a lot of pets and wildlife on the island, have been acting peculiar these past few weeks. Cracker isn't just morose and distant, as usual; she's turned nasty." He looked at Marjorie. "I also have a little schnauzer, Simon, who just lies in his bed all day and hardly ever eats. My cat, Bernice, has run away; no one's seen her except for a flash of her here and there on some neighbor's property. And as for my parrot"—he held up his bandaged hand—"well, you can see how she's behaving. They have literally been biting the hand that feeds them."

"Have you taken them to the vet?" Charles asked, concerned. "There could be a disease going around or something."

"No. No disease. The vet has checked them. It's the same all over the island, though nobody seems that upset by it but me."

Marjorie, not fully sensing the seriousness of the situation, quipped, "An animal revolt, perhaps?"

Timothy kneaded his forehead and sighed again. "I'm afraid it's worse than that. Animals are sensitive to…stimuli… that humans can hardly sense. That's not to say people can't be affected, too, even if they don't know why. There's been a rash of stabbings and assaults in Honolulu and Waikiki. And attacks on tourists by the *kamaainas* in the western part of the island. Every night it's like a full moon."

He explained about the island situation for Marjorie's sake. "There's always been resentment between the native islanders and the affluent whites who build exclusive resorts the natives can't afford for the benefit of wealthy mainlanders. Because of this tourists have often been warned to stay out of certain districts, particularly near the Makaka valley and Waianae mountains. But lately the problem has become worse, much worse. Several new assaults have been reported almost every day. It's like an evil spell has come over the whole island."

He saw the uneasy look on Marjorie's face and quickly added: "I'm sorry to frighten you. Here you are looking forward to a vacation, and I'm giving you all these horror stories. But I assure you it's still possible to have a wonderful time if—"

Charles interrupted him brusquely. "Wait a minute! Maybe this 'spell' you're talking about…"

He stared into space for a moment, blinked several times, then turned to Marjorie with an expression of somewhat reluctant enthusiasm on his face.

"Marjorie, *this* could be what Steven was warning you about." It was as if a light bulb had gone on over his head. "Yes, yes, they could be related. And to think we found this out almost right after we got off the plane…"

Timothy's expression was only one of bemusement. "Charles, what are you talking about?"

Charles reached out and grabbed his friend by the shoulder. "Tim, I think the three of us had better have a good long talk. *Now.*"

They sat down over coffee and sandwiches and compared notes, and as the afternoon grew later and later and the peacocks began their nightly chorus of squeals and screeches, the whole incredible story began to take a frightening shape before them.

* * *

Central Oahu

Linda Kendall drove through the darkening twilight in her rented car and sped past the seedy bars and grocery stores of Wahiawa, one of the least appetizing areas she had seen on Oahu since coming to the island with her husband for their annual vacation. George would think she was crazy for going off like this, leaving him back in their Waikiki hotel room sleeping off his dinner like a sunburned, pot-bellied log, but she was never one to fight back any impulse.

They'd been trying to have a child for the past seven years. George was sweet and blamed himself; the doctor said his sperm count was low but not so low he couldn't impregnate a woman. Perhaps it was all just bad luck and lousy timing; she didn't know. But Linda was sure, absolutely positive, that she would conceive during this vacation. They'd made love, wonderful love, every single night since they'd arrived. One of those nights she thought something special might have happened. And just to hedge her bets she had this silly little plan...it was so silly she hadn't even told George.

She'd read in the guidebooks about the Place of the Sacred Birthstone in Kukaniloko, the remains of an antediluvian "maternity hospital" where, in an epoch so long ago it was almost lost to history, women of royal blood had come to give birth to their children. She knew it was spacey, but she had always believed in astrology and kismet and karma and all that Shirley MacLaine kind of stuff, and maybe, just maybe, if she went out and visited this birthstone, maybe if she prayed and absorbed its magical energy, it would bring her and her husband good luck, increase her fertility, and make this vacation that most marvelous one of all. She was thirty-seven—if she wanted to give her husband a child there was not much time to waste.

She'd talked to her priest, prayed to God, but she knew that consoling words and prayers just weren't enough. Surely there was nothing wrong in what she was doing? God, Father Craven, would understand.

She remembered what the book had said: look for a dirt road to the left after leaving Wahiawa. She didn't expect to find many tourists to follow now—they'd be resting from their luaus or drinking in bars near the beach—but the road was bound to have a sign of some sort. *There!* That turnoff ahead must be it.

She turned into the lane and drove for several minutes past a vast pineapple field until she reached a small grove of eucalyptus trees. She parked in a gravel clearing to one side of the grove.

Taking her flashlight with her, she got out of her car and proceeded along a narrow *ala* until she saw what had to be the birthstone in the middle of a clearing.

There was no one else around. She went over to the stone —upon which the women would lay as if it were a delivery table—and touched the hard surface. The stone was large and flattened and protruded about three or four feet above the ground. She closed her eyes. *Please, oh please*, she prayed—*if there's any magic here let it enter me. Please. I want a child so badly. George and I want a baby. Please—fill me with your magic.*

Then the most peculiar thing happened. She could swear she could hear the sound of a woman gasping, grunting and breathing as if she were actually in the middle of giving birth. Linda opened her eyes.

And cried out in shock.

There was a naked woman, wearing only a ceremonial headdress, lying on the slab; rivulets of sweat ran down the woman's face and body and something was thrusting, seemingly by itself out from between her legs. What made it worse was that Linda could see through the woman, which meant that she was standing beside a ghost or phantom, that Linda was looking into a long-dead past that no one of today should have been able to see.

As the vision grew brighter and took on more substance, the princess's attendants materialized to comfort the groaning woman; they bathed her head and washed down her body with water and cooling ointments. *This was crazy! Unbelievable!* Linda couldn't take any more. She screamed.

Her heathen, heretical prayers to nameless Hawaiian gods had done this—she was so desperate for a baby that she had forgotten her One True Faith, turned her back on years of Catholic training, and was now seeing the result of her thoughtless action. *I meant no harm*, she prayed, this time to God, *forgive me I meant no harm.* But her heart was caught in a terror that made her rapidly back away from the transparent spectres and bolt for her car before any more phantoms could appear to mock her, before she could see any more of this dreadful pagan spectacle.

But as she turned around she saw that already more phantom figures had surrounded the clearing which the birthstone was in, that they were herding her in, surrounding her, their dark red eyes all staring malevolently into her own. She darted away from the birthstone and ran into the field of *halakahikis* over to her left.

Have to get away, have to get away, they're coming for me.

Devils, demons——her terrified mind clutched at every superstition and horror-movie folktale it could think of. She had
prayed, without thinking, to a pagan god, and now the laughing, triumphant Devil would claim her for his own. She had to
pay the price—God had disowned her. Seeing those phantoms, the first supernatural experience of her existence, had
sent Linda Kendall's mind hurtling down an irrational path
from which it would never recover.

A few minutes later, she simply collapsed and fell down
into a puddle in one of the rows of dirt leading through the
pineapple field. She lay there in a heap, panting and crying.
After a moment she trembled with renewed panic, convinced
that the phantoms were still coming after her. She pulled
herself up to her knees and began crawling, nearly insensate
with terror, off the path and into a clump of spiny fruits and
the spiked flowers from which they were growing. The spines
cut into her knees. *Oww, oww, oww!* she said without hearing
herself or even realizing she'd spoken aloud. Startled by the
pain in her lower extremities, she tried to get to her feet, but
something was holding onto her. Something was in her hair, on
her clothing, grabbing onto her arms and legs. She was being
held by *hands:* dozens of hands. There was a dreadful whis-
pery movement on her lips and cheeks, and a grinning
hideous face stared right into her own.

No, it wasn't hands that were holding her. It was *webbing.*
Yards of sticky, fibrous webbing. And she knew what was
walking across her face and what was looking into her eyes.

Earlier she and George had walked through other
pineapple fields, spotted some of the positively *enormous*
spiders that nested among the plants. But they'd been told the
ugly arachnids were harmless, harmless to the fruit, harmless
to humans. They were big and scary but presented no danger.

The face that was now nibbling on her own belonged to
the largest spider she had ever seen and *it wasn't harmless.* She
tried to pull the creature off with her hands, but she couldn't

wrench free of the webbing or the flesh-gobbling, pincerlike jaws. She felt sharp, stinging sensations, pricks of terrible agony, as the spider bit her and unleashed its venom into her skin. Then out of one uncovered eye she saw past the spider's legs to see that a few dozen more of its fellows had come to join it in its feast.

A few dozen?

The field was alive with *hundreds* of crawling spiders.

Every one of which was making its way toward Linda.

CHAPTER SEVEN

Pearl Harbor—the next morning

I'm here, I'm actually here, Marjorie thought, as she and Charles and Timothy and a few dozen other people sailed across the bay in Pearl Harbor in a launch toward the U.S.S. *Arizona* Memorial, a long, rectangular bridgelike edifice that lay directly above the remains of the ruined battleship. *I'm here where Steven died.* Hardly anything else was registering on Marjorie this morning: not the light breakfast they'd had in Timothy's kitchen, the short drive to the harbor, or any of her surroundings—the bright green grass that grew all the way down to the water's edge, the naval bases, airfields, and parking lots in the distance, the large, long white markers with black bottoms that floated here and there in the bay and upon which were painted red letters spelling out the names of the sunken ships in the water below them. She thought about Steven and held back her tears. She was nearly overcome with guilt.

Why didn't I wake up that morning after our night out on the town? Why didn't I wake up so I could have held him and kissed him good-bye, wished him good luck? Instead, she'd been fast asleep and he'd had to leave her a note, a note she had kept all these years and still had somewhere in her house back in Brooklyn. *Why didn't I go ahead and take the money my parents offered me to fly out to San Diego when he was on leave before transferring to Pearl Harbor? Why didn't I go?*

But she had asked herself these questions hundreds of times since 1941, and had told herself repeatedly that she couldn't have known what would have happened, that the flight would have been so expensive, that her parents had already done enough for her and Steven.

She should have gone; she should have forced herself to wake up that morning while Steven was dressing. *But she'd been so tired.*

And now it was too late.

It was too late and she had come here on a fool's errand, come here to confront her greatest loss and relive her pain all over. In spite of what these two men said—these two weird old men—she knew Steven was dead, *was dead*, in every sense of the word, and nothing could ever bring him back again. She would have known if he were alive, she would have known it the moment she set foot on the island. She had been so agog with the beauty and grandeur of Oahu, the excitement of the trip, the awareness of love and sensuality so recently reawakened, that she had overlooked the obvious. She got no *sense* of Steven in this place, no sense of him at all. She agreed to accompany these two old men to the memorial against her better judgment—it was not just a grave, but a grisly death place—and she doubted it would do any good.

Sensing her discomfort, the two men with her were mercifully quiet, staring out into the water or watching the other people on the boat. Tourists, young children, honeymooners—what did they understand of Marjorie's pain? What did any of this mean to them, those ice-cream-smeared youngsters with their yuppie parents who came out here to observe dispassionately a bit of history? What could it possibly *mean* to them? To Charles or Timothy, even? Timothy had confided that although he was over forty at the time, he'd volunteered to work at a desk in army intelligence during the war, a clerk; Charles never mentioned what he was doing at all. How could they understand what she was going through?

She was so tired. She hadn't had any sleep last night. She was glad that at least there hadn't been any dreams, which she had half convinced herself had been psychotic episodes brought on by old age and loneliness and nothing remotely supernatural. She'd been kidding herself. All night she'd had this pounding headache, and those screeching peacocks…She was so tired that everything that was happening this morning had the distant, hazy quality of something occurring under the influence of alcohol.

Against her will she found herself thinking back to their conversation of the night before. Timothy's absurd hypothesis that the island had recently become the focus of demonic activity, that something "evil" on a grand scale was taking place and getting worse, and that it was only the harbinger of holocaust on a virtually gargantuan level. And Charles, so admiring of his older associate, had told Timothy about Marjorie's dreams of her late husband entombed in Pearl Harbor and the implicit warning they seemed to carry. The two men had immediately seized the opportunity to link the two things in their minds. So now Steven was not just "alive" —now he was warning the world of an impending supernatural disaster, of an invasion of a monstrous supernatural being from a world beyond imagining. Marjorie would have laughed in their faces if she'd had the energy.

Her headache, of course, as they explained it, was merely to block "transmissions" from her husband. Apparently the dark monstrous figure of her dreams was "scrambling the airwaves" to prevent her from getting Steven's "message."

The inmates have escaped the asylum, she thought.

And the way the two old freaks had become so animated

as they talked about this upcoming disaster and her late husband and The Significance of It All! They were like demented children discovering a new toy or game, picking wings off flies, and Marjorie was the fly, the pitiful fly who'd been snared by the smooth voice and romantic ministrations of a slimy spider named Charles Emerall.

She had begun to realize why he was so damned interested in her. It was not her delightful mind, nor her body, nor her mischievous sense of humor—it was Steven. Charles was as interested in Steven as Marjorie was; she saw that now. He was using her just as she was using him. He had no interest in her as a person; he was only fascinated by her nightmares and bizarre spiritual sensations. Marjorie was a chemical equation, and he, the scientist. Charles had been hooked the moment she confused him with Steven that day outside the Chinese restaurant.

He and his friend had made such a big deal out *of that*. The fact that she had actually mistaken Charles for her late husband was a sign, an omen that Charles was fated to play a part in the struggle to come, that Charles's and Marjorie's fates were inextricably linked. Well, to hell with all that. And to think she was actually beginning to care for the man. He was just using her, she was convinced of it. *What a fool I am,* she thought bitterly.

The breeze blew across her forehead and brushed a strand of hair across her face. She moved it away with her hand. Charles was peering at her with that sensitive look of his, but she ignored him. She was stronger than anyone suspected. With the life she'd led, she had to be.

And so frightened, too, she had to admit. The things that they said last night!

Timothy told her of his experiences with the occult, told her how he had actually spoken to the dead, seen demons rising, helped exorcise human souls, and sent creatures from the netherworld—"minor demons only," he said—back into the void from which they'd come. And to think she had actually believed him.

But that was last night and this was now and she would rather think he and Charles were crazy and she was a fool than to believe in demons and monsters and that Steven had been *alive* down there in that sunken ship *for the past four decades...*

No, it's not possible. Put it out of your mind, Marjorie.

She thought of all the incidents Timothy had spoken of, the news reports from the Hawaiian papers: crazed animals, nervous pets, the wildly soaring crime rate. Undeniably it added up to something weird, something scary, but still...

No, no, you mustn't think like that, she told herself. It can't be true. It can't be true.

What scared her most of all was that underneath this show of strength and anger *she felt it, too.*

She repressed that thought, isolated it, sent it hurtling right back into the furthest recesses of her mind. She was a rational twentieth-century woman, she told herself, nobody's fool. She didn't know why she had let herself be talked into coming out here on this dismal gray morning—why she was letting herself be *used* this way—but now that she was here she'd go through with it and be done with it once and for all.

Steven.

The launch was slowing down. The once-distant white memorial was now only a few yards away and she could see the large rectangular entrance at the side, the ramp with the banister that one walked up to get inside the building. She started shaking—not from fear of devils or demons or nightmares, she assured herself, but from the knowledge that she was not walking into a cemetery but into a morgue, that within seconds she would be standing not just above Steven's grave, but above the very place where he died...It would be like looking down at the site of an accident to look for leftover bloodstains. These morbid people were coming here to get some kind of thrill, *to see some blood*, and she was—suddenly— very ill…

But before she could say anything she was walking up the ramp with the two men on either side of her and there was no turning back.

* * *

Although Charles had visited Timothy in Oahu about six times during the past twenty years, he had never gone out to see the *Arizona* Memorial and regretted not having done so before. This was history, a tribute to the dead, and he was quite impressed and saddened by the display. He was very concerned about how Marjorie was taking it—after all, her husband was still down there and she could not be as impersonal about it as other visitors. Whether Steven's soul was trapped or not, whether he was in some way living or was irretrievably deceased, there was still part of his presence beneath this memorial, part of his essence and his memory. They had recovered only seventy-five bodies from this ship after the brutal Japanese sneak attack, and more than eleven hundred were still down there in the ship. It was terrible to contemplate, gruesome and sobering. For a moment he felt as if this was an invasion of privacy, a morbid enterprise, but he knew it was also one way of honoring and remembering the war dead. He supposed that made it all right.

He wanted to hold and squeeze Marjorie's hand and tell her it was okay, but she pulled away from him. Ah, well, he could understand—she was here to honor her husband and it was no time to commune with other men. He could understand. But it hurt. And he wondered if what he felt for Marjorie and what he thought she felt for him would be jeopardized by this trip. (They laughed at the elderly, the world laughed; it thought the elderly's grasping for love was "cute" and their need for sex ridiculous. Yes, he was old but he still had feelings, still needed companionship and more!) Surely Marjorie realized that even if Steven's soul were down there in the remains of the *Arizona*, even if they could manage to free that soul, there was no way the two could ever be reunited in *this* life. Was she aware of that? Or had she come here with expectations that could never possibly be fulfilled?

She'd been pulling away from Charles since they arrived on the island. The plane trip had been fun, even romantic, but the feelings on the flight seemed to have been all but erased. She slept in Timothy's guest room last night—or at least tried to—while he used the couch in the living room. He'd been hoping she would come out and ask him to be with her, but it never happened. Even Timothy's pets wouldn't go near Charles.

Of course he recognized that Marjorie was very disturbed by what he and Timothy had been discussing last night. Timothy was a true psychic, not just someone interested in the occult, as Charles was, and the reverberations he felt indicated that things were much more serious than Charles had imagined. Both he and Marjorie, he suspected, were in way over their heads. Still, Timothy had suggested that a trip to the memorial might be advisable. He could tell Marjorie had reconsidered it and was reluctant, but to her credit (and his discredit, he supposed) she had consented to go along with them. He wondered how she was taking all this. She looked so tired and pale and would not speak to either of them since they'd entered the launch. He would let her go off by her lonesome if she wanted to.

Timothy, off to one side by himself, seemed quite absorbed in something, not necessarily the memorial, so Charles did not bother him either. He concentrated on studying the contents of the enclosed bridge on which they were standing. There were three separate chambers: a small museum displaying the ship's bell and other items; an assembly room, where ceremonies occasionally took place; and the shrine room, where

Charles studied the marble wall listing the names of all the dead crewmen. Some of the children and vulgar, chattering tourists who refused to walk about in hushed respect were quite offensive to Charles, but he held his tongue. What could he expect from loud, overdressed Americans whose most sensitive act was to cheer bloodshed at soccer games and whose most intellectual pursuit was to watch television sitcoms? He turned away from a particularly obnoxious gaggle of couples and went over to one of the large glassless wall openings located on either side of the assembly area. (There were also huge open wedges in the "ceiling.") He stared out into the water and looked down.

The one-hundred-eighty-four-foot-long memorial, which spanned the width of the ship, was closer to the prow of the *Arizona* than to the stern, and never came into contact with the ship itself. The rusted top of the *Arizona* was only a few inches below the clear, pale blue water. Charles felt himself getting teary-eyed at the thought of the tragedy and all those wasted lives and wondered what Marjorie, who was lost in the crowd, must be going through. He looked out at the large brown funnels that stuck out slightly above the water level. It was said that the oil that still leaked out of these funnels was the tears of the dead sailors…

If he tried hard Charles could imagine how it had been that day: waves of Japanese planes flying across the Pacific, converging on Pearl Harbor from around both sides of Oahu; the first bombs dropping on Ford Island in the bay; airfields assaulted by both dive bombers and fighters, their incendiary bullets blowing parked American planes to pieces. Then the attack against the Pacific fleet's eight battleships; inboard ships blasted by high-level bombers, while torpedo bombers concentrated on the outboard ships. The planes flew past the wreckage in the harbor, strafing the ships in an attempt to finish off any survivors.

The *Arizona* was hit the hardest—with the most casualties,

the greatest damage—and it was unsalvageable. The sneak attack must have been unbelievably horrifying to witness. All those ships, all those people dead in a matter of seconds…Human beings committed atrocities against one another that seemed more demonic than anything conjured from the netherworld. At least a murderous demon wasn't killing its *own kind.*

Yet underneath his feeling of sorrow and futility, Charles felt something else, something even darker, if possible, and more hopeless. It could be merely that Timothy's words of last night were affecting him, or that he was affected by those same reverberations to which Timothy had been referring. He didn't know.

He was startled out of his reverie by a commotion over at the other side of the assembly room. Someone was crying, wailing—it was a whine of agony and grief, an outcry of pain and loss and unacceptance—it sounded like a young girl…but he knew it wasn't. Rather the cries of a young woman's *memory* coming back to her with a force and clarity that was utterly cruel and just as inevitable.

People were looking about, coming into the assembly room to see; others, embarrassed, were turning away. Charles brushed past everyone in his path, past the Good Samaritans who were reaching out to offer aid and comfort to the bereaved, and saw exactly what he was afraid of and expected to see.

"Marjorie," he said.

She was standing by the side of one of the big open spaces that looked out onto the water, her back to the harbor, tears dripping down her face and her hands clasped together in front of her, up near her eyes. She was shivering and her face looked young and frightened and totally helpless. She saw Charles and seemed to recognize him. Without saying a word, she cried out for his help. She did not speak; Charles did not speak—there was no need. A great eloquence passed between them—an eloquence that spoke of wasted years and lost loves and pointless bloodshed, which reached from the battered brown remains of the ship down there beneath their feet and struck straight and true into her heart. An eloquence of human contact and compassion that required no words, ever.

He bundled her lovingly into his arms and let her keen, let her grab on to his warmth until she was quieter and the choking sobs had receded to a dimmer, yet still-wrenching flow of sorrow. He took her out of the assembly room and over to the exit from the memorial.

Charles shook his head in self-flagellation. They should never have brought her here.

He would look for Timothy later.

* * *

Timothy had been only a few feet from Charles and Marjorie as they passed by but he hadn't seen them. Although he had visited the memorial once before and found it infinitely depressing, never had he picked up such an amazing amount of psychic residue. He had assumed he'd never picked up individual "thoughts" from the ship that first time because even then so many years had gone by since the war; either there were no ghosts, no sensations, left to receive, or rather there were so *many* sensations from so many dead, from so much violence, that it all became jumbled into a headache-inducing symphony of turmoil with all "signals" canceling out the others.

But now it was as if a presence that was down there on that ship, a form of energy—no, *two* forms of energy—were suddenly, slowly, emerging. These presences had been down there since the attack on Pearl Harbor, he was sure, but only in the past few weeks had they awakened from their dormant state. He was certain it was this event that was responsible for the odd happenings on the island! He stood there in the middle of the assembly room and tried to lock onto these presences—he sensed they were in conflict and yet somehow linked together—but they resisted him, fought him off; or at least one of them did, at any rate. They had evaded his psychic probes all along, but now that he knew where they were—if not *what* they were—it was a different story. The more he probed the more his head hurt. The more his head hurt the harder it was to probe.

There was no doubt in his mind that this had something to do with Marjorie Russell and her entombed late husband. It would be too much of a coincidence otherwise, and he didn't believe in coincidences, had learned never to believe in them. Besides, he had sensed something about Marjorie almost from the first. Her presence on this island was of great importance; something wanted to reach out to her—but something *else* wouldn't let it? Thank God Charles had called him when he did. If the two of them hadn't come to Oahu…

What was it? he wondered. *Who was it?* "Kanaloa," or whatever he might call it? Or something worse? Something so monstrous that just thinking about it gave him the tremors.

And then something happened. He felt a lessening of the pressure in his head, and something gave in, something gave way. *There!* Now he was receiving signals, now he might learn what was happening. He braced himself for what might follow.

Argh! He felt a blast of both heat and cold and doubled over in pain as if punched in the belly. A few people standing nearby came over to offer assistance, but he waved them away and managed to stand up straight by himself. And then:

He was hit by an even greater psychic assault and this time he tumbled to the floor before anyone else could move.

He was running like mad through a corridor of twisted, smoking metal. Men were screaming and crying and there were bodies of sailors both dead and unconscious littering the floor. The whole ship was slanting to the right and it was hard to see. Nobody even knew where to run to. A stream of water was gushing down the passageway and it was hard to breathe. There was a loud wrenching groan like the world coming to an end and a booming thud on the port that spelled torpedo.

Someone was screaming that the forward part of the ship was completely wrecked, that a bomb had hit the forecastle, exploded in a forward magazine, and caused dozens of fires and additional explosions. Hundreds of men were already dead. The captain was dead. Rear Admiral Kidd was dead. The ship was sinking, the ship had sunk, the ship was even now settling on the bottom of the harbor. Another lurch—and he went sprawling. His hand reached out to steady himself and slid across a smear of blood on the wall.

No, no, I don't want to die.

"We're trapped," somebody screamed. A burst of flame erupted from a cabin and two men, their hair and clothing on fire, screeched about in agony as the stench of cooked meat hit the air. There was nothing anybody could do but watch in horror as the sailors revolved and danced and contorted in mindless desperation until nothing was left but ashes.

One part of Timothy's mind observed: They're just boys, just frightened boys. They haven't done anything to anyone.

Steven-Timothy continued down the corridor, past shouting men, stepping over unconscious bodies, wanting to help but afraid to stop moving, overwhelmed by panic, seeking an exit, seeking proof that they had not settled on the bottom and didn't have volumes of crushing water between them and the surface. The thought of being on the bottom of the harbor cut off from life-giving air, surrounded not just by steel and iron and fire but by...Hopeless, it was hopeless.

Steven-Timothy found a buddy of his lying half in, half out of a doorway. He helped him to his feet, dragged him down the hall, following the others, wondering if anyone knew what they were doing. Another lurch, his friend fell away from him, fell under a flood of boots taking up the rear. Steven screamed. Oh God. *Terror grew and overcame him. Another lurch and a thud. More smoke, fire, an explosion that sent a shudder through the entire ship. Then the water came in, tons of water, and he thought—good it will put out the fires—but of course it was worse than that, the water swept him and all the others off their feet and suddenly he was drowning, burned and crushed and bleeding, banging off bulkhead after bulkhead, dying, and with one final breath he cried out Azarüb Save Me You Promised!*

Timothy woke up and found himself lying on the memorial floor with concerned faces peering down at him.

"Are you all right?" asked someone who helped him to his feet.

"Yes," he said, but he really meant no.

How could he be all right! How could anyone be all right?

He had lived through Steven Russell's final moments and learned what had happened then, and, more important, what had happened *before*. He *knew* what was happening on Oahu.

And he was terrified.

Azarüb.

For as bad, as tragic, as it had been, what had happened in Pearl Harbor on December 7, 1941, would pale in comparison to what was going to happen on Oahu in the not-so-distant future.

* * *

Makua—40 miles from Honolulu

Douglas Rumbarton was having such a great time scuba diving off the coast of Oahu that he had almost forgotten about sharks.

Diving instructors practically sneered at him with contemptuous laughter when he mentioned his fear of bumping into a shark while underwater. They assured him that there weren't many sharks in Hawaiian waters, and their pupils rarely if ever ran into one. Nevertheless, people had seen an occasional shark in the ocean off Oahu and he was petrified at the thought of encountering one. Great white, mako, tiger shark—it didn't matter; he found all kinds of sharks quite terrifying.

Most people took solace in the fact that shark attacks on humans were so infrequent—even in shark-inhabited waters —that one's odds of meeting up with one, let alone being killed or just bitten, were astronomical. Still, even if only two or three people got killed each year, somebody had to *be* those two or three people. And *they* had probably thought they were safe, too, had reassured themselves with the statistics about infrequency of attacks and all that, and still they'd gotten eaten. So much for the odds.

Douglas was not scared of sharks due to silly Hollywood films with their polyurethane shark models chewing on nubile actresses. He was scared because two members of his immediate family had had encounters with sharks. When Douglas was a boy his father proudly used to show him the wicked scar on his leg where a shark bit into him in the South Pacific. He had narrowly escaped being devoured. And Doug's younger brother Ernest had had a scare off Long Island's Jones Beach back in the sixties when a shark attacked his sailboat and nearly got him. He also learned that his mother's cousin Matilda had disappeared in the 1940s while sailing off Bermuda at about the same time that a marauding great white had been observed in those waters. And a great-uncle named Mortimer had reportedly choked to death after eating some shark meat in a seafood restaurant.

Jinxed, his family was jinxed. Sharks were out to get them.

What fascinated and frightened Douglas was that Hawaii —where he'd come with his wife, sister, and brother-in-law for a month-long vacation—was a land full of native superstitions about sharks. According to Hawaiian folklore, sharks had minds like men, and could even transform themselves into human beings and walk on land. One afternoon while visiting Pearl Harbor he had learned that the first disaster actually to occur there had taken place way back in 1913, years before the Japanese attack on U.S. naval forces. Just as it was nearly completed, America's first dry-dock at the harbor tumbled into ruin when the foundation collapsed. The Hawaiians said it was due to the wrath of Koahupahau, Queen of the Sharks, who was angry because they had dared build the dry-dock right over a cavern where her brother lived.

Douglas was sure if he spoke to some of the old-timers they'd tell him that his fear of sharks was entirely warranted. He was convinced that sometime in his family's past one of his ancestors had angered a shark god, and every now and then the shark god's minions would get even by picking on one of the offender's descendants. Such as Douglas. It was something for which he just had to watch out.

Yet the world down here offshore was so serene and beautiful that Doug forgot about his silly fantasies and began to relax. He had gone diving several times already with an instructor and other students, and also completed three dives all by himself. One was supposed to stick to the buddy system, but neither his wife, sister, or brother-in-law—who only wanted to drink beer and stuff themselves with roast pig —had any inclination to dive along with him. Besides, he *liked* being alone. It was so, well, liberating...

Since there had been no bad incidents on his previous dives—and no sharks—he felt secure enough today to face his fear and swim into the famous Kaneana Cave, a large opening in a solid stratum of solidified lava and coral that was said to have once been the home of Kaneana, a shark god who could change into human form at will. (Doug was sure he'd spotted a few sharks-in-human-form walking around the island—as well as down in the Wall Street district of Manhattan, where he worked.) Shark god or no shark god, he was going to enter this forbidden cave and confront his fear and superstition once and for all, banish it forever. He would go back to New York City A Man Transformed.

As he approached the entrance to the cave—he had reconnoitered earlier—he saw a variety of tropical fish: the *menpachi* or squirrel fish; the *manini* with the black vertical stripes that gave them the nickname of "convict fish"; the funny-looking *uhu* or parrot fish. Out in deeper waters on dives with his class he had seen *ahi* (tuna), *mahimahi* (dolphin), and a variety of turtles and squid at a distance.

He found that once he got a grip on his fear, diving in the *kai* (salt water) of the *moana* (ocean) was almost a celestial experience; he saw a new universe of sights and colors, fantastic underwater volcanic vistas like the underside of an alien landscape, bright coral colors, streaming plants, and small fish of every shape and variety to delight his senses and tickle his imagination. He had never suspected it would be so glorious. There was nothing down here to fear; only a rare, precious wonder that was meant to be revered and respected. He was glad he had come here by himself. The presence of other people would only have spoiled it.

He swam over to his right, near the undersea cliff or *pali* jutting out from the volcanic rock all around it, and swam into the entrance to the cavern. He turned on his seaworthy flashlight so he could see clearer, and his eyes widened at the somber, lonely beauty of the cave. The only one inside, he felt a sense of awe and isolation that was as gratifying as it was unnerving.

But the solitude had a negative side, too, in that his mind began to work backward, and in this anxious stream-of-consciousness state he began again to think of sharks and gods and vendettas. *He thought of rows of slashing teeth, fish that walked as men; he saw gaping jaws clamping down on his body parts as he screamed in terror and defiance.*

He was giving himself the willies. He decided he had been in here long enough and did not feel like exploring any longer.

Feeling like a coward, he began to retreat; he was too spooked to argue with himself or to try to reevoke his courage.

He turned around, came to a dead halt.

A dark massive shape was between him and the exit from the cave.

Doug's heart began pounding. Inside his mask his lips opened and issued a muffled, strangled scream.

It was the largest shark he had ever seen, but it was more than just that. There was a foulness about it, an unnatural aspect, something obscene and abnormal in its glare, in its all too human eyes, and in the funny-looking appendages underneath that resembled grasping hands or claws. The shark had lips that seemed to grin and chuckle as it advanced.

But sharks didn't have *hands.* They didn't have *lips.*

This hybrid monstrosity of shark, man, and demon continued moving toward Douglas, whose mind whispered *Kaneana, oh, God, it's Kaneana* even as a more sensible part of his brain was screaming denial and rationalizations as fast as it could come up with them.

Douglas had somehow managed to back up to the far end of the cave when his oxygen tanks crashed into the rock wall and the shock of the impact reverberated all along his body. The flashlight flew out of his hands and he felt himself sliding helplessly to the bottom of the cave. He screamed and trembled as the dark shadow, the enormous teeth, loomed over him and descended, descended, until there was nothing left but blackness and blood and a turmoil that led inevitably to an endless silence.

CHAPTER EIGHT

"Steven Russell's spirit is alive and mentally active down inside the hull of the U.S.S. *Arizona*," Timothy said. As if to bely the seriousness of his words, as if clinging to safe, commonplace things were the only way to deal with it, he quietly took a puff on a pipe in his mouth—his only vice, rarely practiced—and blew a whoosh of aromatic smoke into the room. "There's no mistake about it."

They were sitting in the upstairs dining area, nursing drinks, or, in Marjorie's case, a cup of coffee. Huddled around the table, exhausted and frightened, they looked like three refugees who'd landed in another country without money or baggage. It *was* another country they were in, a whole new world where demons walked and dead men invaded nightmares. And if Timothy and Charles were unsettled, Marjorie was all but hysterical.

"I sensed something while I was on the memorial," she said now, staring off at a circular pattern on the wallpaper. "That's not why I collapsed, no. That was because of the memories, the awful thing that happened to my husband, down there…" She paused a moment to collect herself. "But underneath my grief and hysteria I did sense something.

Sensed someone watching me, pulling at me…" She shoved her fingers back through her hair and shook her head. "Or maybe I'm just going crazy."

"You're not going crazy, Marjorie," Timothy said. "When I was pulled down into Steven's mind, into his memories, the last moments of his life, I, too, sensed a lot of things. I sensed that I had not tapped into psychic residue, but into a *living mind*. Not necessarily living in the way that you and I are living, but alive, wakeful, extremely agitated and conscious. And I sensed *another* presence, one that was almost *fused* with Steven's. And I also picked out of Steven's mind what happened, what he did to wind up in such a regrettable position and…it's incredible. In the brief time that my own mind linked with his—due to his efforts, I expect—I learned *everything*. And I learned what it all has to do with the negative energy enveloping Oahu."

They had returned to the house immediately after leaving the memorial, each of them silent and contemplative on the drive. In the backseat, Marjorie had allowed herself to be cuddled by Charles, who stroked her hair and whispered soothingly as she shivered in his arms. He had decided to take her directly to the waiting launch and stay there until Timothy exited the memorial and joined them. Marjorie remembered little of this; somehow they had gone back across the harbor in the launch, disembarked, made their way through the parking lot to Timothy's car. She had been absorbed in thoughts of Steven, just as Charles was absorbed in thoughts of her, and Timothy in thoughts of what he'd learned while out in Pearl Harbor. Now that they had relaxed and made themselves comfortable back at the house, it was time to discuss what was happening.

"A spell," Timothy said. "Your husband cast a spell the night before he left for basic training."

"A spell? But that's impossible. I was with him all—"

"While you were asleep. He did it in the empty nursery."

Yes. Marjorie remembered the odd fragrance in the room, the markings on the floor...

"He knew a lot more about the occult than he ever let on," he told Marjorie. "He actually knew enough to conjure a demon."

Marjorie protested. "A *demon*. I can't—"

"Marjorie, I know you're skeptical and this is all a lot for you to take in, but please let me just get the story out and then you can ask all the questions you want."

She sat back miserably in her chair. "Go ahead."

"He called up a demon from a netherworld and made a pact with it. If the demon promised to protect him from all harm during his period in the service, he would allow the demon to use his human shell for that same period of time to experience the pleasures of earthly existence. Steven was afraid of dying, you see. He didn't want to die in the war." Timothy wiped his lip thoughtfully and added with a show of sincerity, "He wanted to come home to you and the baby."

Marjorie suspected that Timothy was just telling her what she wanted to hear, but she was nevertheless grateful.

"Steven knew how much demons loved taking mortal form, as it were, on occasion, and frolicking 'harmlessly' on earth. The demon agreed to Steven's proposal and let some of its essence or psychic energy take up residence inside your husband. Steven's mind was still in control, as it was supposed to be."

He paused to take another puff on his pipe.

"But that day, December 7, the demon, as demons are wont to do, played a particularly 'mischievous' trick on Steven. While the bombs burst and ships sank and metal and fire and bodies flew everywhere, while hundreds were killed, the demon *did* protect Steven—but only in its own peculiar fashion. He put a protective aura around Steven's body, which, until recently, put Steven into a state of suspended animation. I said a moment ago that I sensed Steven's 'spirit' down there, but the truth is much more startling. Steven's mind *is* down in that ship, *not* because he is a spirit who has been tied to his place of death, but because, in essence, he *is not dead.*"

When Marjorie heard that, her eyes popped open and she almost started to cry—but she said nothing. *She would just sit quietly for the meantime until the man explained himself fully and she was positive that he had actually said what she thought he'd just said.* She wanted no misunderstandings, no false hopes. She would just do as he said and *listen.*

"In the meantime," Timothy continued, "the demon—or at least the demon's *mentality*—has continued to inhabit Steven's body, while it uses its energy to pull itself, *all* of its energy and physical being, that is, into our dimension. Back in 1941, of course, it used the surprise and panic of the sneak attack to take over Steven's mind, and the energy released by the bombs to contain him. It's all very complicated and makes you wonder: Could the demon have protected Steven from, say, a simple knife thrust, when there was no great energy expended for it to absorb and use? Realistically, under normal conditions it may not have been able to do much for Steven, to protect him, at all. Things turned out differently, much differently, than your husband expected. Perhaps differently than the demon expected, also."

He threw in another aside: "What Steven conjured back in your nursery that night, by the way, was only the demon's image or aura, sort of a holographic projection into our world —not the actual creature itself." He paused again to blow some more aromatic smoke into the room. It seemed scented with cherry or cinnamon. "You see, the demon didn't just want to walk around in a human form for a while; no, sir; it wants dominion over our entire world. The demon is, in effect, an alien lifeform, what some might refer to as one of the Dark Gods that walked our earth in centuries past, and who were somehow banished by early man, and who now have no other desire but to reclaim our world and have their way with us."

"*Stop!*" Marjorie threw out her hand and tried to catch her breath. There was only one thing on her mind. "Steven isn't dead? Is that what you said? My husband *isn't dead!*"

Timothy nodded. "Yes, that's what I said. Steven is alive."

Marjorie had trouble adjusting to, accepting, the *enormity* of it, *the implications.* "He's just been 'sleeping' all this time?" *She couldn't believe it.*

"More or less, yes. Until recently. Just as the demon is partially in our world, Steven is partially in the demon's universe. Time moves at a different rate there. Forty years is however long it is to the demon—to gather its strength for total emergence. But the more it takes over Steven's mind and body, the more Steven fights it, the more alert—and, conversely, subjugated—Steven becomes. The demon's dimension is related to, or may even be, what we on earth call the astral plane. In spite of the fact that he is not dead, not a spirit, Steven has been able to communicate with you through spiritual means. Through your dreams. The result of being merged with the demon is that Steven's psychic power was increased a thousandfold—he thought of you, the person he loved the most, and even in his subconscious state, he reached out to you. But the demon kept fighting him, kept trying to subdue his mind entirely as the demon wrenched itself from its world into ours. That's why all you've ever received were jumbled messages, garbled dream images. The more 'awake' Steven became, and the more the demon pulled itself into our world, the more intense your dreams became. Don't ask me to explain it in any logical, rational manner, because I can't. We are not dealing with a logical, rational world or occurrence any longer."

Marjorie could hardly keep track of all her reeling thoughts, could not possibly come to terms with them. It was fantastic, intoxicating, even a little bit scary. Steven was *alive,* actually alive. There was still hope. Charles was right: He had not been in mental anguish all those years; most of the time his mind had only been sleeping, dormant. She was full of hope and joy and incredible excitement.

Then: *But some demon is using him, trapping him, a* demon *is about to emerge into our world.* She felt faint again. She put her face in her hands and waited until the dizziness and sense of futility receded. Why did everything good that happened in her life have to have such an insane, rotten underbelly?

Charles leaned toward her. "Marjorie, are you all right?"

"Yes, yes. I'll be fine. It's just…so fantastic, so much to take in." Her tears now were tears of joy, tears of fear, mingled together. She felt as if she were being twisted in twenty different directions, each of which led someplace else and yet interconnected a dozen times along each path. Nothing made sense anymore and she was panicky and frightened.

"What will happen if this demon is successfully able to enter our world?" Charles asked Timothy.

What will happen to Steven? Marjorie wondered.

Timothy rubbed his eyebrow and put his pipe down on the table. "Steven and the demon are now engaged in a tug-of-war, which Marjorie saw, in a figurative sense, in her nightmares. Neither of them is winning, but the demon has a distinct edge. Until now. I could tell that Marjorie's presence on the island, her nearness to him, has caused a ripple effect in the reverberations emanating from the ship. Steven knows she's here and is crying out to her to stop the demon, to help him fight it. But the demon also knows she's here and will do whatever it can to *finish* her first."

Charles clearly didn't like the sound of that. *"What?"* He nearly knocked over his glass in his agitation. "What can we do? Nothing must harm Marjorie."

Timothy tried to calm him but only half succeeded. "I'm only being blunt, Charles, because Marjorie must understand what terrible danger she's in. In fact, it might be best if she were to leave the island."

Marjorie didn't waste a second registering a protest. "No!" she said. "I won't go! Steven needs me."

Timothy picked up his pipe again and began to lift it to his mouth, but stopped when it was halfway there and instead gestured with it intensely. "Listen to me, you two. The demon's slow emergence is already affecting everything on the island: the wildlife, people's minds and tempers. And it's only going to get worse. The demon uses and expels tremendous amounts of energy as it comes from one world to the next—the whole delicate fabric of reality is being subjected to a kind of torsion. And the creature is also feeding on the psychic pain of visitors to the memorial, as well as the fantasies and subconscious desires and hatreds of the animals and residents all over Oahu—its influence extends *that far.* And it's the demon's influence that is stimulating them to violence and madness even as it uses the energy of that madness to help it free itself.

"Pretty soon, if not already, the planes of existence will begin to curve out of alignment; they'll merge together at random places and we'll see odd lifeforms—dangerous, malevolent lifeforms—inhabitants of other worlds, poking into our own. Not to mention the *materialization* of our fears and nightmares, our darkest desires, which is not at all beyond the demon's power. God only knows what the creature will do when it arrives to those of us who survive this first wave of its attack. The demon will have a thousand ways to try and destroy you, Marjorie, if it doesn't force you—or Charles or me—to destroy you ourselves." He swore, pushed away from the table, and began to pace the room like a panther. "It is just too dangerous for her to stay."

"Wait a minute," Marjorie said. "A minute ago you made it sound as if my being on the island was *bolstering* Steven, making him fight harder against this demon, isn't that true? If

Steven is strong enough, bolstered enough, can't he resist the creature and send it back where it came from?"

Timothy nodded thoughtfully, then said, "Yes. Yes. Possibly. But I can't really be sure."

"And my very nearness gives Steven strength? So much strength that the demon sees me as a threat?"

"Yes."

"Then it's settled. I'm staying. Besides, if you're really as knowledgeable about the occult as you claim to be, if you know so much about this creature and what it wants just from one…link-up…with Steven's mind, why can't you come up with a counter spell to send that horror back where it came from, with Charles's help?" She looked at Timothy, at Charles, and back at Timothy again, blinking away tears. "Don't just stand there!" she said. She pointed toward Timothy's well-stocked study. "Go look in those…those books of yours…and come up with something *fast,* for God's sake!"

Timothy's lips pulled back in a grimace of futility. "All I know is the demon's name. Azarüb. One of the most power-ful, most malignant, of the Dark Gods of legend. Why Steven *was foolish* enough to—"

"Can he be stopped?" Charles asked.

"I don't know. Before I knew this evil force's name, I referred to it half jokingly as Kanaloa, the Hawaiian counter-part to Satan. Well, I wasn't far wrong. Azarüb is supposed to be so all-powerful he might as well *be* the Christian devil. Because when he gets here, it *will* be the end of the world. Look what he's doing already, and he hasn't even fully emerged yet."

"How was Steven able to summon such a powerful demon?" Charles wondered aloud.

"Accident, mostly," Timothy said. "Although the various items he used in his ritual seem nonsensical by our standards, by the laws and sciences of the netherworld they *were* capable of drawing forth that dimension's inhabitants. Azarüb answered the call, that's all. Not only was Steven the first human foolish enough to enact the ritual in eons, but he was also the first whose sensitive, imaginative nature allowed him to perceive the beast's aura and communicate with it. Just as I alone on the island have sensed the reverberations playing all over Oahu."

Charles looked as if all energy had been drained out of him. He slumped back in his chair and said, "Timothy, what can we do at a time like this? We can't contact the police, call in the National Guard, send out the army. Are we really the only three people standing between Azarüb and his invasion of the earth?"

"Yes, we are," Timothy said.

"We three...and Steven."

And each person in the room knew exactly how utterly hopeless the odds were.

* * *

Western Oahu

This simply could not be happening in this day and age, Melanie told herself, but it was happening, and no matter how hard she prayed and screamed and closed her eyes wishing it would all go away, it was happening to her and it was happening right this minute.

They had surrounded her at one end of the supermarket parking lot just as she was putting the key in the door of her rented car. The next thing she knew she had been bound with rope, a handkerchief stuffed down her throat, and thrown into the backseat with three or four other people—not captives— while somebody up front started the car with her keys and drove off at a fast, screeching clip. There were at least two or three more people in the front seat with the driver, all squeezed in together, laughing (or was it snarling?), and twisting their heads around to talk to those in the back who were sitting on top of her. They were dressed in wild outfits and their faces were painted. They looked like Indians, savages; she suspected none of them was much older than she was, barely twenty.

She hoped this was just a childish prank, a joke the locals liked to play on tourists. She hoped they'd have their fun, give her a good scare, and then let her go back to the house she'd rented with three college roommates. She was so scared she wet herself; she was afraid if they smelled her pee it would only make them more contemptuous. She had heard how much some islanders hated tourists. As it was, someone kept cuffing her viciously on the back of the neck and then slapping her on top of the head. She felt a few punches, kicks in her ribs. *Where were they going?*

A short while later she was dragged out of the car and tied, like a pig or calf, by the arms and legs to a long yellow pole that several of them carried between them. The gag fell out of her mouth and she started screaming, pleading with them to release her, but it did no good. She saw, even from her upside-down, blood-to-the-head vantage point that some of them were women—at least they wouldn't allow the guys to rape her, would they? Then again, what could she realistically expect from the kind of women who would hang out with creeps like these?

They started up a steep trail into the mountains. Melanie thought she recognized a few landmarks, though she was so hysterical this didn't really register until somewhat later. She had come up this trail before with her friends. Eventually it dawned on her that the trail led to Kaneaki Heiau, a temple that had originally been dedicated to Lono, the god of agriculture, but in the late seventeenth century had been a *luakini heiau* where human sacrifices were performed. *Human sacrifices!*

But that was ages ago! Hawaii was civilized, these people

were sophisticated—she recognized the designer jeans and expensive shoes beneath the gaudy costume tops—there were no sacrifices on Oahu anymore. This had to be a joke, a bunch of drunken kids, that was all it was.

But the kids didn't seem drunk—only wide-eyed and barbaric—and on closer inspection she saw that many of them were a lot older than she'd at first thought, as old as her parents, even. Her brain took all of this in without consciously realizing it, and while it did not enter her thoughts in any concrete manner, it did on a certain level contribute to her terror.

The journey took a couple of hours—with frequent rest stops when her pole was briefly lowered to the ground—but to Melanie it seemed a lifetime. She was hoarse from screaming and so nauseous she thought she'd throw up. Could terror become so all encompassing it was almost sublime? She wished they'd just kill her and get it over with, kill her and put an end to the terror.

The temple consisted of two thatched huts in a clearing layered with wood rose vines and snow creepers, two impressive prayer towers, and, of course, the altar, which was exactly where the merry band was heading. Melanie renewed her struggle, trying to pull out of the ropes, which cut so painfully into her ankles and wrists, but her writhings were ineffective. She wept copiously, shuddered in her confinement, and begged them to release her. She could hear the caws and chatterings of the area's wild birds, the gentle rhythmic gurgle of the nearby stream—a sense of peace that belied the horror she was now experiencing.

These people are crazy, they're crazy, they're going to kill me. Kill me! Why didn't anyone help her? Why hadn't anyone seen these people and what they were doing to her?

Then she heard a commotion behind her and saw a group of racing figures heading in the direction of the gathering.

Thank God—police, concerned residents, security guards, somebody, anybody, who would save her—

But these people hadn't come to save her.

For they had that same mad look in their eyes.

Instead of rescuing her, attacking her captors, they joined the others and added their own pitch of excitement and anticipation to the general level of hysteria, which moved the original group of worshippers to move even faster and with more fiendish, demented energy. Melanie was rushed over to the altar and the pole she was tied to was lowered to the ground. A man pulled out a wicked-looking knife and used it to slash the ropes that bound her to the pole. Figures moved in to grab her, to rip off her clothing and throw her down onto the altar stone. The back of her head hit the solid rock with such impact that she nearly lapsed into unconsciousness. She tried to keep from blacking out, pulled herself back into a fully conscious state, and then was sorry she had. *She was naked and it was chilly, and she wished she could have covered her breasts.*

Squirming, contorted figures were dancing about in the enclosure. Paint-smeared, weirdly clothed individuals, men and women of all ages, lifted their heads and hands to the sky and cried out to the Hawaiian war gods Kukailimoku and Kuwahailo —Ku, the snatcher of land, and Ku of the mouthful of maggots. She saw that taking up the rear of the assemblage, which now numbered over one hundred people—all of whom had covered the distance up from the valley below either on foot or on horseback—were tall, strong men who carried enormous effigies of these gods: great wooden heads that were ablaze with yellow and crimson feathers, which had mother-of-pearl eyes reflecting the light of numerous fires and burning torches, as well as gaping maws that revealed sharp rows of canine fangs and smaller teeth.

Impossibly she was caught in the middle of a Hawaiian ceremony of the seventeenth century! And she saw that many of the orgiastic celebrants seemed to be transparent, like phantoms, that half of the pagan congregation was ghostlike, as if comprised of specters from the past. But the others were real enough. She could feel their flesh-and-blood hands holding her down, clutching her arms and legs, preventing her from doing much more than wriggle uselessly on the stone like a speared and flapping fish. *This cannot be happening!* she screamed silently.

"Kukailimoku! Kuwahailo!" the celebrants hollered at the sky. The fires flared, the smoke thickened. One of the thatched huts caught on fire, flames licked at the bottom of one of the towers, which began to glisten and smell like sweet, cooking meat. Melanie heard screeches of agony. The revelers seemed to be unaware of what was transpiring. Someone's headdress caught on fire. Melanie saw bodies tussling, tumbling, fornicating in the dust and on the grass. A great flock of wild birds took flight out of the forest. The several men and women around her, her kidnappers, were momentarily diverted by what was happening all around them. One of them, a middle-aged woman with a hard face and tiny coal-black eyes, seemed to wake up out of her trance and look about as if wondering what she was doing there.

Melanie seized the moment. She tried desperately to reach the woman's hand. "Help me! Help me!" she begged. For she realized that both of them were caught up in something that went far beyond the normal laws and sciences, that had little —or everything—to do with the islanders' antipathy toward the white man.

But then the woman's perplexed, horrified look was replaced by one that was again stern and unforgiving.

The woman lifted her knife and quickly slit Melanie's throat, then her belly from sternum to pubis.

She lifted out Melanie's internal organs one by one and handed them to her companions. They held them up to the moon for approval.

Then began to eat them.

CHAPTER NINE

It was before the witching hour, but Timothy and Charles were already exhausted. Marjorie had wanted to stay up with them, but it was obvious that her mind wasn't able to concentrate—not that anyone could blame her—and besides, she really didn't know what to look for. The men sent her to bed with their blessing. Timothy and Charles had gone through almost a third of Timothy's vast collection of occult writings. They'd unearthed several references to the great Azarüb, but absolutely nothing that would provide some clue to a way of sending him back to his own dimension.

"Not only can I not recall if I ever came upon anything like it," Timothy admitted, "but even if I did, I wouldn't remember exactly where. Azarüb has always been sort of a myth, one of the supreme giants or deities that hover in the background but which hardly anyone has had any experience with. This is so frustrating." He looked about his study, which was a large cluttered chamber with several bookshelves filled to overflowing, two desks awash in a sea of papers and folders, and two long tables each holding what appeared to be a ton or two of extremely large, dusty tomes. "I should have catalogued all these books years ago. Hired someone to put in a filing system. So much information. And all of it useless…" He sank into one of the few chairs in the room that wasn't covered with books or parchments. "And now when we need this information so desperately, when it could be literally at our fingertips, I can't find it." He kneaded the back of his neck and let out a groan.

"Have you found anything in Melvale's book?" Timothy asked his younger companion. "He's known for putting in bits of information which seem useless at first glance—as if he were inserting notes for some other person's book in his own —but later turn out to be quite helpful. It would be just like him to have the secret of saving the universe buried in some chapter about poltergeist infestation or telepathy with the dead."

Charles stood up from where he'd been bending down over a large book he had opened on a table. "Nothing yet. Trouble is, the really good stuff is never in the index." He flipped a few more pages while Timothy shuffled out of the room to get them more coffee. By the time his friend returned, he had finished that book, leafed discouragingly through another, and was now well into a third. "Azarüb," he muttered, "they have plenty on every other demon, but none on the granddaddy of them all."

His pedantic mind took over and Timothy heard himself saying, "Not necessarily the granddaddy. One of the seven or so higher demons, I'd say. Not even the strongest, but strong enough. I've never encountered anything more than a lesser demon myself. That time in Beirut, the governor's son—the boy who'd read those parchments and become obsessed with…ah, well, that's in the past. All it took was a little compound of salt water and absinthe to get rid of that one. Poof. It was gone. And even that crone in Hungary who spoke in tongues and grew a tail—she was possessed by a demon with a penchant for killing animals—even she was exorcised simply by reciting a few lines of forgotten poetry.

The rules are so odd, Charles, so odd. Sometimes I think my success has all been due to sheer, simple luck and nothing more. Just luck. And the gods and devils and demons or whatever you want to call them are looking down on me and laughing."

Charles sipped his coffee and blew on it to cool it. "I keep thinking of that poor man, Marjorie's husband…down there with that thing. He's awake now. Can he feel torment? Can he feel pain?"

"Torment, yes. As Marjorie's dreams have proved. Physical pain? That I can't say. Hopefully not. But you're right, for that boy's sake we must do everything we can—" He turned back to Charles and his face wore a tense little grin. "Of course, if we don't succeed it won't matter to Steven or to anyone else. There won't be any world left. Not the world as we know it, at any rate. Everything will become chaos, a holocaust, everything will change forever…"

For a few moments neither of them said anything.

"Before we continue," Charles said finally, "I want to check on Marjorie."

"I just did," Timothy told him. "She's sleeping peacefully. Perhaps Steven will leave her alone now that he knows what she's doing for him."

"You think he knows?" Charles answered his own question. "Yes." He smiled tenderly. "Such a brave woman."

"A woman in love," Timothy said. He looked down at his hands awkwardly and then back up again at Charles. "Can you handle that?"

"Timothy?"

"I mean, can you handle the fact that this woman you obviously care so much for is still in love with her husband?"

Charles shrugged. "But he's—"

"Dead? No. Not the way I see it. Didn't you hear me explain it all this afternoon?"

"Yes, but…can he be brought back to life, real life—life like you and I have, physical form, walk about like you and I do—if we defeat the demon?"

Timothy's stare was still intense. "It's possible."

"And if we don't defeat Azarüb?"

Timothy looked as if he didn't want to answer. "Steven will die along with the rest of us." He looked over at the window. "Or perhaps the beast will keep him alive for playful reasons, use his body to walk about in on its mission of mayhem and domination. I can only guess." Again he stared intently at Charles for a moment. "Are you having second thoughts about helping me, knowing that if we defeat Azarüb it will possibly mean the end of your relationship with Marjorie?"

Charles bristled. "Timothy! Of course not. How can you say such a thing? Yes, I'm a lonely old man, but not so miserable and pathetic that I would allow the world to die to preserve a brief relationship that would only be destroyed in the resulting conflagration anyway. Do you have such contempt for me, Timothy?"

Timothy held up his hands in apologetic supplication. "Of course not, old friend. Of course not! It's just...it's just that the demon feeds upon doubt and weakness, perverts strengths into faults, it finds and exacerbates vulnerabilities. Even now——I can sense it—people are dying on this island. Good people, innocent people. Not just at the hands of animals or murderers, but of visions, things, monstrosities from their own imaginations, from out of time, from other worlds in the nether dimensions. Everything is in a state of flux, out of control."

He slammed his hand down on a heavy, encyclopedic volume and swore in anger and determination. "Let's get back to work, Charles. We must find that information." As he reached for another book he looked as if he were struggling to suppress a shudder. "There'll be no sleeping, no safety for any of us, until we do."

* * *

Western Oahu

They called it a wasteland and that was a perfectly apt description. Jerry had never had such a sense of desolation in his life. For miles around there were jagged volcanic rocks, choppy smears of ancient solidified lava trails, a hard rugged terrain that proved challenging even to the Jeep in which he and his two buddies had driven. He tried several times to get comfortable in his sleeping bag, but no matter which way he turned or swiveled, he'd always feel some rock or bony outcropping sticking into his back or stomach. He wondered if he would get any sleep at all that night. It was cloudy, too, and while the breeze had not turned into a wind, he was afraid it might rain or even storm before morning.

The others were quiet enough. Bernie was a few feet away snoring; Clark was lying behind the Jeep out of sight, but Jerry couldn't tell if he was sleeping or not. Well, Jerry couldn't blame *them*—he'd been the one to suggest this camping trip. Let their girlfriends stay in the luxury hotel with the maid service and modern conveniences, he'd said; he and his buddies would set out to see the real Oahu that the tourists missed...while the girls soaked up the sun and drank Margaritas and mai-tais on the beach. Shit! He sure could have used a Mai Tai right then.

They'd set out the day before yesterday, camping here and there, driving right to the very tip of the island, it seemed, down to Yokohama Bay Beach, where the Farrington Highway ended. Regular cars could never have continued the trip on the road that remained, not over a landmass that looked like something from another planet, a potholed lunar landscape with fissures and crevices and sudden rises and drop-offs. Even in the Jeep the going had been difficult. They had finally stopped when night fell, and in the meager illumination of their headlights and cloud-filtered moonlight they got the unnerving sensation that the road had turned into a narrow promontory stretching out into the ocean and that if they kept going they would drive right off the end of the island. The nighttime created the disquieting illusion that instead of being on solid ground, they were surrounded on all sides by nothing but water. When the bottom of the Jeep clumped against a hard bumpy surface and they bounced so high on the seats that the three of them were nearly thrown out onto the road, they decided it was time to call it a day.

Luckily they had prepared sandwiches earlier; there was no way they could have made a fire with no wood and little vegetation. The only thing they saw were all these little puka shells that the natives collected in bunches and sold to tourists. The breeze from the shore nearby was cool and pungent and what little moonlight escaped the clouds glittered across the water. They saw a lost, lonely boat sailing past an outcropping shaped like a bosom, and, far in the distance, the automated lighthouse at Kaena Point. Jerry wanted to drive out to see the satellite tracking station at the point in the morning. They ate in silence, a bit awestruck by the vast deserted surroundings that stretched out in all directions. It really did seem as if they were at the end of the world.

All in all, Jerry would rather have been back at the hotel in bed with his girlfriend. He had a persistent erection and really felt a need to masturbate, but he felt vulnerable and exposed out there in the open. He was sure the other fellows wouldn't see him if he nestled down deep in the bag, but that wouldn't leave his fingers or his dick enough room to maneuver. He knew he wouldn't be able to sleep until he'd relieved the pressure, though.

He stared up at the clouds and tried to forget about the ache in his groin.

A few minutes later, while he was entertaining himself with assorted erotic fantasies, he heard an odd sizzling sound coming from his right, away from the Jeep and out in the darkness.

He sat up in his sleeping bag and tried to peer into the gloom, wondering what could be making the noise. Next he heard a crackling, thudding kind of sound, as if clumps of earth were being overturned and rocks chiseled into pieces. An earthquake? He sat up straighter in the sleeping bag and wondered if he should wake Clark and Bernie.

Then he saw a light issuing from over where the noise originated. Odd—it was as bright, brighter, than a flashlight, and it seemed to be coming right from the earth itself. It was as if a fissure had opened in the ground and was emitting a ghostly illumination.

Weird.

Jerry was very frightened. He heard no voices, no vehicular sounds, saw no one walking in the affected area. Maybe it had something to do with the tracking station. A beam from a ship or the lighthouse? Or could it be a geyser of phosphorescent water? he thought. That's all they needed, the three of them, to be scalded to death by a sudden spray of boiling white water. Talk about terminal sunburn.

He tried to joke about it but it was freaking him out. The light was getting stronger and stronger, and he heard scrabbling sounds coming from deep down in the earth. He jumped to his feet. No way was he dealing with this by himself. "Clark! Bernie! Wake up! Wake up! Something's happening, guys. Something crazy!"

When he was sure they had heard him and were stirring themselves from their sleeping bags, he swooped up his flashlight and started walking toward the mysterious light source. He heard more popping, crackling sounds and saw chunks of dirt flying in the air, as if some burrowing creature were hurling them out of its path on the way to the surface. He didn't quite understand where he was getting the courage to proceed as every part of him was screaming "Go back! Go back!" He had almost reached the first fissure when another opened up a few yards away, emitting a fresh flow of brilliant white radiation. He got scared—the ground was liable to fall away beneath him any minute.

A hairline crack in the surface of the road about seven feet away from the Jeep and from Clark started to move in a zigzag course, widening, toward the car.

"Guys!" Jerry screamed. "Come here! Come here quick!"

The beam from Jerry's flashlight was swallowed up, dissipated in the light from the fissure, so he turned it off. Just as he reached the crevice he saw something—something large— moving through the light. It had a smell like hot motor oil and fresh excrement with an undertone of rotting vegetable matter. It shambled over the rocks like a large lumbering ape or scrabbling insect.

The creature from the crevice was a large, hulking monstrosity with insectile features, constantly moving mouth parts, scales and claws and a hump on the back. It had large protruding eyes, perfect circles, with gleaming red dots in the center of a gelatinous mass. No nose or ears to speak of. It made no sound except for an expectant ear-splitting buzzing as it skittered rapidly toward Jerry.

Jerry backed up from the creature, tripped on an outcropping, and fell to the ground.

He heard a noise of groaning metal and looked over his shoulder to see the Jeep disappearing into another enormous crevice that had opened up under the road. Clark was floating high above the crevice, as if he had sprouted wings. Then Jerry saw the great misshapen paw that held the young man aloft, saw an underslung jaw and dripping fangs that opened wide to clamp down onto Clark's shoulder.

Bernie was almost halfway between Jerry and Clark, frozen in motion, clearly not sure where to look or which friend to help. "Run, Bernie, run!" Jerry screamed.

A stew of saliva and blood and torn meat fragments

dropped out of the grinding maw of the second creature chomping on Clark and fell into the crevice.

Jerry's stomach convulsed. He turned back toward his own pursuing monstrosity, and rapidly got to his feet when he saw how close the thing was.

Bernie was rushing toward the jeep in a panic. He stopped when he saw the creature munching on the mutilated, headless remains of Clark Barrow. He turned abruptly and ran alongside the road heading back to the Farrington Highway some miles distant.

Jerry was running in the same direction as his friend when he saw Bernie abruptly disappear as if snatched out of the air by some science fiction program's teleportation beam.

The crevice. Bernie had fallen into the crevice where the Jeep was.

Jerry heard Bernie screaming.

First checking to see that his own pursuing demon was still a relatively safe distance behind him, Jerry ran over to where his friend had disappeared, and peered into the fissure.

The crevice seemed to have no bottom. The light was nearly blinding. Jerry had to squint and partially cover his eyes to see anything. It was as if a million-watt klieg light were shining up from a subterranean soundstage. Every crust of dirt, every niche, every furrow in the rock was lit up and washed out like the wrinkles of an old woman sitting in front of her makeup mirror.

Bernie was holding onto a ledge that protruded from the wall about three feet below the ground. He was holding on with only the last three straining, desperate fingers of his right hand. "Help me! *Help me!*" he screamed.

Trying to maintain his balance, Jerry reached over to help his friend. If he were to fall...

Just as Jerry's hand grazed the very tips of Bernie's fingers, the latter lost their grip on the rock and Bernie plummeted down, down, down, into the infernal light that blazed so intensely, the light that would serve to burn the image of Bernie's endless plunge into Jerry's retinas for the remainder of Jerry's life.

Which wasn't very long, as the two demons, and several others from other sinkholes, converged on him from out of the darkness. *These creatures had come from other dimensions through warps in the space-time continuum caused by Azarüb's emergence,* but Jerry didn't care about that. He was too busy screaming as they raised him off the ground, tore him apart, and systematically devoured him in only a matter of seconds.

* * *

Is this a dream? Am I really lying in a bed in Oahu, sharing a house with two men who tell me that my Steven is alive? Is this bed, these walls, this sheet, these memories, real? Or am I still back in my house in Brooklyn, having a deluded, lunatic fantasy that's somehow taken on shape and substance?

Marjorie lay in the bed in the guest room and tried to sort out her feelings. She was exhausted, but couldn't sleep—she'd only pretended when Timothy looked in on her—which only made thinking more difficult. Everything about this was so hard to accept. Yet she clung to the notion that everything Timothy said was true because it meant that her beloved Steven was *alive*, and might be brought back to her whole and intact.

She thought nothing about the ramifications of this; nothing mattered but having Steven with her in the final years of her life. It was not too late to make up for lost time: not too late to love and be loved. Even her brief episode with Charles proved that she was still a complete woman, that Steven would want for nothing. He would need her, desperately need her, to help him adjust to the fact that he had been stripped of nearly fifty years of existence. She was afraid that the joy he would feel at his release from Azarüb's power and the terrible confinement of the ship would almost be vitiated by his remorse at coming out of the ordeal an old man when once he'd been young. *But, Steven, we'll both be old, both of us. I'll show you what the world is like, how much it's changed. I'll be your guide, your soul mate. It won't be so bad, being old, it won't be so bad for either of us as long as we have each other.*

And Charles? She hoped Charles would understand. She owed him so much. A sense of being alive that he had awakened in her, a sense of being wanted and cared for. If it hadn't been for Charles, if he hadn't come when she wanted him... everything would have been lost. Steven. The whole world, too, perhaps, if what Timothy said was true. Everything might still be lost. She felt a stab of guilt for lying there idly while those two men were so busy outside, but they'd insisted she'd only get in their way.

She supposed it *was* significant that she had mistaken Charles for Steven; it had been the great turning point. Had that not happened; had she not fainted; had Charles not taken her into the restaurant...she would still be in Brooklyn, suffering terrible nightmares—much worse, even, than they had been before—and Steven and the world would have had *no hope.*

She could lie there no longer. She had to get up and do whatever she could, even if it was only to provide moral support. Of course, part of her wanted desperately to fall asleep so that she could "talk" to Steven, communicate with him in that extraordinary way of theirs. This time her dreams would not frighten her. But, then, there was Azarüb to consider... She would hate to see Steven suffering, struggling like that, tortured in that awful demon's hand. Perhaps it was better to remain awake... Yes, for now it was better.

She had just gotten out of bed and put on her robe when the door opened and Charles came in.

"I'm sorry. I just wanted to see if you were all right," he said. "Can't you sleep?"

She tightened the cloth belt around her robe and brushed the hair out of her eyes. "It's all right. I'm getting up. No, I can't sleep, and I'm tired of lying here looking at the ceiling." He stepped aside as she moved through the doorway and into the hall. She turned back to look at him. "There must be something I can do—even if it's just make coffee."

He reached out and touched her shoulder and beckoned her back to his side, where he stood in the doorway.

"What is it, Charles?" she asked.

He put his arms around her and drew her close. It felt right, an old friend's affection, yet it bothered her. "I just want to hold you a minute," Charles said.

Marjorie felt much more than fondness emanating from him; she felt a kind of desperation, an outcry of loneliness and need. *Oh, Charles, why did you take so long to come into my life? And why now? Why did you have to be the very man who's helping me get my husband back?*

After a moment Charles released her and looked down at her face. "Is something wrong, Marjorie?"

"Things are...Charles, things are different now. Steven—well, Timothy said Steven's alive. My husband's alive. It...it changes everything, can't you see? I—you've given me so much, Charles, so much. Without you..." She reached up to touch Charles's face tenderly. "But Steven...Steven has to come first, you see."

Charles's expression was unreadable, but he nodded gravely. "I do understand, Marjorie. And I very much hope that we can succeed in helping Steven, in helping to reunite you with Steven. I know if we don't succeed there may not be much of a world left for us to..." He held out his hand in an impotent gesture. "I only wanted to say, if things don't work out, well...I want you to know I'll be here for you, Marjorie." He bent to kiss her cheek. "I'll be here for you."

She started to speak but he hushed her, put a finger to her lips. "Don't say anything. There's no need to. I understand completely. Come and sit in the study with us while we read. You'll be our inspiration, okay?"

As they walked along the corridor Marjorie said, "I tried to recall things Steven used to say about the occult, but nothing comes to mind about any demons or alternate lifeforms. I don't think I ever heard him mention Azarüb. I've wracked my brain..."

"We'll find something, Tim and I. Keep your fingers crossed. We'll manage to free Steven somehow." His brow creased with determination. "I know it seems impossible—but mankind has been around for a hell of a long time and I don't think we're about to throw in the towel because of some ugly, nasty creature who doesn't even belong here, are we?" He saw the confused, hesitant look on her face. "The human race can mess things up on its own perfectly well, don't you agree?"

She smiled ruefully. "I'm afraid so."

Neither could believe it was really happening; hence, they had difficulty imagining Azarüb, something they had never seen, never touched—except in Marjorie's nightmares—being triumphant.

When they walked into the study they found Timothy on the phone, agitated, animated, his eyes bulging and fingers shaking with impatience. During a lull in his conversation with whoever was on the other end of the line, he turned to the others and said, "It will take us too damned long to find the information we want—and there's no guarantee I even have it. So I've thought of something else. A desperate measure, perhaps, but better than nothing.

"You see, Steven is still basically in suspended animation —only his brain is working. And since the demon hasn't yet fully emerged, he can't animate Steven's body, either. What I propose, therefore, will be risky—quite risky—because of Azarüb's developing *mental* powers, but I can't think of anything else."

He had their undivided attention. "We're going to go

down and get Steven's body out of the hull of the *Arizona.* And once we have his body..."

He leaned forward and looked at each of them in turn. "I'm going to exorcise the demon."

Thunderstruck, Marjorie and Charles could only stare blankly at each other.

* * *

Eleanor Josephson had made this pilgrimage to Pearl Harbor about every five years since the memorial had been erected in 1962. Nothing would stop her, no one would deter her—not her children, not her husband, who knew how much the trip drained her and wished she'd let go of her war dead—for she had made a sacred vow the same day the telegram arrived at her house saying that her brother had died on the U.S.S. *Arizona.* She had vowed that she would never forget Roy Barnes, that she would cherish the memory of her eighteen-year-old brother for as long as she was alive, and even her marriage to Roy's best friend, Lyle Josephson, and the birth of four children, wouldn't displace the spot in her heart that was reserved exclusively for Roy.

Lyle accompanied her on most of these trips to Oahu unless he had a business conflict. She brought her children as soon as they were old enough to make the trip. They grew up seeing pictures and hearing stories about their Uncle Roy, the blond freckle-faced "troublemaker" who actually had the sweet soul of an angel. Eleanor found it difficult to stand on the memorial knowing Roy's crushed remains were buried somewhere below in the mud and the silt. She found it diffi-cult to imagine what his last horror-stricken moments must have been like. He was only a boy, *only a boy.*

They said nowadays that one was a man at eighteen, an adult, but as far as she was concerned that wasn't true. One had barely tasted life at eighteen, barely begun...

Lyle was down in the lobby of the hotel buying cigarettes. The two children who'd accompanied them on this trip —Susan, who was forty, and Peter, who was forty-three— were out to dinner with their spouses. They were good children to come with her to pay homage to an uncle they had never known. She knew it was just a vacation as far as they were concerned, especially her son-in-law and daughter-in-law, but at least they were respectful. They had wanted her to go out with them that night, to shake her out of the doldrums, but she'd had a particularly rough time at the memorial that afternoon and wasn't much in the mood for merriment.

Each time she came to Oahu she would go to the memorial every afternoon except Monday, when it was closed, for an entire week. She would pray for Roy, and weep for Roy, the whole time. Somebody had to remember, she told herself, somebody had to care about these forgotten men.

She had nothing against the Japanese she saw on Oahu, many of whom hadn't even been alive at the time of the attack, but it was funny that all these years later the Japanese and Americans were friendly, as if nothing had ever happened, as if no one had ever died. But of course the Japanese had Hiroshima and Nagasaki to remember. She imagined they had memorials—bigger memorials—over there. And she was sure that business interests—wasn't it always money?—dictated that Japan and the United States be allies. She was glad that was the case, of course, but was struck by the irony. All those men died fighting a war between nations, and now those nations got along just *swell,* and the men—the dead men—were simply gone and forgotten. There were no good times for them. No love, no joy. *No existence.*

She started crying again.

Roy, oh, Roy. I loved you. And I miss you. I still miss you, Roy.

She thought of how she used to play with her baby brother when she was a little girl. She remembered him sitting at the beach in his high chair playfully throwing pebbles at her, running around in his cute little cowboy outfit. She recalled their first trip to New York City when she was twelve and he was eight. Mother had said, "Eleanor, you must watch over your brother. There are a lot of people in New York and he might get separated from us. We're counting on you, Eleanor. Watch over little Roy, okay, sweetie? That's a good girl." And they'd given her a pat and some candy.

But Roy had gotten away from her at one point; he'd pulled away from her when something in a window caught his attention, and she and her parents had a hell of a time tracking him down. "Eleanor, you were supposed to watch him!" She'd nearly had heart failure before she caught sight of him at the corner petting a big black dog and laughing.

She didn't want her brother to go to war. She had prayed there wouldn't be a war. And he was dead before it even began, killed on the very eve of the United States's involvement in World War II, killed in the conflagration that *ensured* the United States's involvement.

Some people said that the government knew about the Japanese plans for the attack on the harbor and did nothing, *that they knew*...but that Roosevelt wanted the U.S. to enter the war and figured no one would object to it once American boys had been murdered...

But of course that was monstrous. Utterly monstrous. She couldn't believe it. *She wouldn't.*

She bent over and reached into the night-table drawer and took out a picture of her brother, taken nine months before his death. He'd had such great plans, that boy. He was a maverick, stubborn as a mule, opinionated, but he had a sensitive side, a quiet side. Had he lived, there was absolutely no doubt in Eleanor's mind that he would have amounted to something, gone on to great things. And now, now...

He had died screaming.

Now he was entombed, dead, nonexistent. *Except in my heart, Roy, you are very much alive in my heart.*

Eleanor took a tissue off the night table and wiped her nose and eyes. She felt so exhausted and depressed. Another trip out to the memorial tomorrow. It would take a lot out of her, but there was no question of not going. She must go. It was the only way she could keep her brother's memory alive. The only way she could honor and love him.

She sensed movement to the right of the bed. Had Lyle somehow come back into the room without her realizing it? The sneak.

Then a voice that sent chills through her—because it was so familiar—cut into the silence and said, "Eleanor. Eleanor, I'm here. Over here…"

She looked over by the bureau, where the voice was coming from. There was somebody standing there. It was —But no, *it wasn't possible*, it couldn't be possible.

Her brother Roy, looking as young as he did in her picture, was standing by the dresser. His left hand was on top of the bureau, supporting him. His face was full of pain. Liquid trickled down from his eyes—tears or just water?—and there was a trail of water and seaweed and rusty footprints leading across the carpet. The lower half of his body was blackened and bleeding, but the top half seemed strangely untouched. The skin looked so smooth, so white. Eleanor could smell a brackish, oily fragrance—also a smell of blood and decay—emanating from the vision. She could see partially through the figure, and knew either her tired, obsessed mind had conjured up a phantom or the ghosts of the dead really did walk the world, after all.

"Roy…?" she said. In spite of her terror she couldn't tear her eyes away, couldn't turn her back on her brother. To find out after all these years that her feelings, her faith, had been true, that one *could* live on after death, meant so much to her. To know that somewhere her brother was at peace, that he was safe and might even be happy and fulfilled.

But he looked so haunted, so sad. And his body…

Awkwardly, haltingly, Roy moved toward the bed. In spite

of her previous feelings, Eleanor froze in horror. Roy looked so…awful. He reached the bed, dripping blood and salt water, and leaned in over her head. Up close she could see that his eyes were blank and there were tiny maggots burrowing through the pasty, decaying flesh of his face. His breath was indescribably foul. "Roy, oh, Roy," she whimpered.

"I hate you," Roy said. "I hate you—*you cunt.*"

When Lyle and the children got back to the hotel room they found Eleanor lying on her stomach on the bed, under the covers, shivering and screeching, her head—gushing tears—scrunched down into the pillow below her. They tried time and again to get her to tell them what was wrong, but she wouldn't say, she just *would not* say, she couldn't say, she *couldn't…*

* * *

In other houses and hotels around Pearl Harbor, other people were being visited by specters of men who'd died on the *Arizona*, mutilated, hollow-eyed specters who whispered obscenities, who told their loved ones things they would never have said, would never have felt, had they been real. These phantoms were *not* the spirits of the deceased, only materializations of the dead sailors plucked out of the minds of the visitors to the memorial. The things they said were not true, were not real—but their victims, their loved ones, couldn't know that. There were some—those who survived the coming holocaust, that was—who would never be the same again.

Azarüb had seen to that.

* * *

In the U.S.S. *Arizona* Memorial in Pearl Harbor, Sam Lewis, the "custodial engineer," had just finished washing the assembly room floor. He put the pail and mop away and went over to one of the wall openings to have a rest and a cigarette. All day the weather had been gloomy, and now it sure looked as if a storm was brewing. Clouds were getting darker, roiling above like bloated combatants made up of felt and steam, threatening a deluge and nothing less. He wanted to finish up and get home before it poured.

What was that? The water out in the harbor seemed to be more agitated than it should have been. A powerful wind had sprung up, sure, but not strong enough to cause such waves and commotion. The red-and-white markers of the other sunken ships in the harbor were moving back and forth, shuddering, almost as if...but that was impossible. Sam thought he could hear a distant groaning coming from below the waterline.

And then the whole *Arizona* Memorial swung violently to the right and Sam went flying to the floor.

He got up, pulled himself together, and ran back to the opening in the wall. He looked down at the ship.

The U.S.S. Arizona *was moving, quivering, tilting to the port side,* and rising. It had risen far enough in the water to butt the bottom of the memorial and slam it to one side. Sam had worked there since 1973 and had never, *never,* seen such a thing happen.

What was worse, he could hear noises coming from the ship itself. Pounding, banging, metallic noises. The noises of flesh on metal, metal on metal. He could swear he heard voices, screeching voices, *the shrieking and clawing of enclosed, scratching fingernails.*

The remains of the *Arizona* tilted to one side, then the other side, rose in the water, fell with a splash...*something inside was alive...*

Old Sam was convinced: The men inside were alive and they wanted to *get out...*

CHAPTER TEN

"You people gotta be nuts!"

Franklin Ugamata was chewing a piece of gum with voracious intensity. He was a thirty-eight-year-old Hawaiian-born Japanese-American who had been a professional deep-sea diver for the past fifteen years. He was small, but broad-shouldered and powerfully built, with slick black hair, a nice-looking face, and a voice and speech patterns that made him sound as if he'd spent most of his life in Brooklyn.

Franklin went wherever he was needed. He had worked on oil rigs in the Gulf of Mexico, cleared out pumps at chemical plants, dived in the thirty-degree temperatures of the North Sea at depths of up to a thousand feet, cleared away wrecks and debris from the bottom of the Mississippi, and worked on broken pipelines and twisted cables all over the world. But he had never, *never*, been asked to participate in something as crazy as this before.

Frank had known Timothy Zacharides for almost ten years. Timothy had often come to Frank's house to have dinner with Frank and his wife, Amiko. Frank respected the man and enjoyed conversations with him. But there was a limit, there *had* to be limits, after all.

"You want me to dive down and get a body out of the *Arizona!* Man, you're crazy!"

Timothy and his two friends explained that this man was actually *alive*, that some demon was keeping him alive, had kept him alive for over forty years. They explained that because of this, his body would still be intact. Timothy—an eighty-two-year-old, for Pete's sake!—would dive with Frank and hopefully be able to direct him to the proper spot in the hull via "psychic" means! Fuckin' *incredible!*

"Even if I did do this," Frank said with a smirk, "how do you suppose I break *into* the hull, hmm?"

Then the other old-timer had given him a hoot. "Aren't there special underwater tools you people, you professional divers, use?" the old guy asked. "Isn't there special equipment you use to break into a shipwreck?"

Frank slapped his knee and laughed long and loud. "First you want me to dive down to the *Arizona*. Then you want me to break into the ship and get a body out. Now you think I'm a one-man salvage operation! Look, that kind of equipment is expensive. On a job like that the equipment is provided by whoever's *hired* me. I don't carry that kind of stuff around." He shook his head from side to side and popped his gum. "Say, Tim, is this some kind of joke, or what?"

"It's not a joke, Frank," Timothy said, and he told Frank all about this Azarüb and netherworlds and demons and disasters and somehow managed to tie it all in with the general weirdness—Honolulu's soaring crime rate, the numerous attacks by wildlife, and other strange phenomena—that were occurring on the island.

After he had heard all of this, Frank sat back in his seat, folded his arms across his chest, and said, "I repeat. You people gotta be nuts!"

"Don't you believe us?" Timothy asked.

"Believe you? I believe *you* believe that crazy story. But me? No, I don't. I don't believe in no devils and demons and monsters, Tim. No, sir. And I ain't about to do sumpin' crazy —and illegal—like breaking into the hull of the *Arizona*, even if I could. Just so you could *exorcise* some guy's body. You been seein' too many movies, man!"

The woman had been sitting in one corner of the room all this time, kneading her hands and practically whimpering. She was old, too–kind of short and dumpy, but with a sweet, pretty face and lovely grayish-blond hair. Now she shot out of her chair and said, "Please, please help us! It's my husband, *my husband*, they're talking about!"

Her husband!

This was getting weirder every minute. Wait till Frank told his wife! And Amiko had always liked Zacharides. Maybe the old guy was getting senile. And these two friends of his from the mainland were definitely *pupule*.

"Look, I'd like to help you. But the bottom line is, I don't got the equipment to break into no ship. And that's a *memorial*, man. The U.S.S. *Arizona!* Breaking into that—why that's practically sacrilege. They'd have my *butt*, man, if I was caught. And no offense, Tim, but I'm not diving with no inexperienced eighty-year-old, sorry."

He got to his feet and started making his way to the door, but they wouldn't allow it. The three of them came at him from all sides, crying, pleading, hollering, and he was really afraid they meant to do him violence. He put up his hands, threatened them, told them to move out of his way. He'd humored them long enough, but now he was getting angry.

And then there was an explosion, the biggest *boom* he had ever heard in his life, bigger probably than all the booms that had resounded on December 7, 1941, put together, a *boom* that he swore must have cracked both the sound *and* fuckin' time barriers, a *boom* that was heard from one end of Oahu to the other and for a moment almost seemed to usher in the end of eternity. Timothy's house rattled and quaked, and Frank thought he could hear people yelling and dogs barking in the distance, not to mention those damned peacocks screeching worse than ever, and a clatter of trees cracking in the ungodly wind that had sprung up and then ceased almost as suddenly. The *boom* lasted only a second or two, but even Frank could sense that its reverberations would last a lifetime. And Frank, a small but strapping man for his race and, if he had to admit it himself, one of the bravest people he knew, just about melted into a big puddle of jelly from the terror.

"W-what the hell was that?" he exclaimed. It sounded as if the boom had originated in Pearl Harbor. Talk about coincidence...

But the worst thing was the look on Timothy Zacharides's face, a look that told Frank that everything the old man had been saying was *the truth*.

"It's too late," Timothy said.

"Azarüb is here.

"Azarüb has left the ship."

* * *

All across the island of Oahu, just when the explosion rent the air, several things happened at once.

In Pearl Harbor, Sam Lewis and the U.S.S. *Arizona* Memorial were literally blown out of the water. The memorial rose into the air a full twenty feet before plopping down into the harbor with a splash that sent giant waves crashing onto the lawns and parking lots on the shore. Sam fell into the water and drowned. Damage to the memorial was minimal, surprisingly, but it sat lower on the water than before, at an angle, a bit bent and battered. Instead of being separated from the hull of the *Arizona*, it now rested directly on top of it.

In the water below the memorial, there was a huge gaping hole in the hull of the ship near the bottom of the harbor. From the hole a black viscous substance like the ship's lifeblood poured out into the water, turning it a sickly grayish-green color.

In the naval base at Pearl Harbor, each and every window was shattered in each and every building. People out of doors were knocked off their feet, some sent tumbling against trees, cars, or telephone poles.

More than two dozen people were killed in that first second.

* * *

The storm that had been brewing on Oahu all day suddenly came into full bloom. Gale-force winds blew across the outer regions of the island, tossing pedestrians around as if they were made of straw, overturning automobiles, sending trees hurtling like javelins through windows, sometimes knocking down houses. A thunderous downpour drenched everything, and jagged bolts of hissing lightning crashed down from the sky nearly to incinerate trees, cars, and people. Black clouds roiled and billowed and a foul odor permeated the island.

* * *

Behind barbed wire at the satellite tracking station at the tip of desolate Kaena Point, all the equipment was going haywire. The computers were down, instrument panels shot off sparks, men and women wound up with burned fingers or scorched clothing. Nothing would register properly and readings were way off. Satellites would blink in and out of view on radar, as if something kept blotting them out of existence.

As if something were blotting out existence itself.

* * *

At the Naval Ammunition Depot in Laulaulie-Maile, officers were busy responding to phone calls and assuring concerned callers that there had not been an explosion at the depot. But no one had the slightest idea of what it was that *had* exploded. After a short while there was too much static on the lines for words to be heard, and a minute after that the phones went dead.

* * *

First it was the birds.

At Diamond Head, the thoughts of even the most sophisticated inhabitants, including members of the National Guard at Fort Ruger, were utterly perplexed, full *of death* and *doom* and *destruction*. After the big *boom* hundreds of dead birds were plummeting like stones from the sky and smashing against rocks and pavement. The variety of waxbills, sparrows, canaries, and finches that inhabited the Diamond Head area either flew about in an uproar, cackling and screeching, or simply dropped dead in mid-flight like boiled descendants of high-flying Icarus. They littered the ground like feathered confetti, flightless harbingers of worse things to come.

Next it was the *trembling*.

* * *

Diamond Head had been dormant for approximately 150,000 years, but that night the floor of the crater trembled and shook as if something below were trying to escape. Pits formed in the gravel and tarmac, and steam rose from cracks and fissures; a great wave of heat bathed the entire crater in an eerie pink glow that seemed positively supernatural.

Last it was the *fire*.

After the pits belched the last of the steam, they turned into geysers, geysers that spritzed hot molten lava out in great tall gushes, setting fire to buildings and to people who had ventured out of doors for fear of the buildings collapsing. It was as if Pele, Goddess of Volcanoes, the twelfth-century sorceress who was killed by a lava flow and returned from the grave as the spiritual embodiment of that lava, had had the last laugh after all.

A laugh that was quickly turning into the screams and tears of the dead and dying.

* * *

In the elegant, Oriental-style estates of fashionable Makiki Heights, residents stepped out of their homes to witness a great flood of biting, scratching, screeching rats—some as big as small dogs—running up from the valley and sleazier districts of Honolulu that they had previously infested, and scampering malevolently all through the neighborhood in a panicky rush to nowhere. These large, ferocious rodents would stop whenever they saw human prey, stop and surround the victim, jump at him from all sides, biting and clawing, until he or she was forced to the ground from weight of numbers and soon covered in a living carpet of voracious animals. The germ-carrying vermin ran into open doors and climbed through windows; they attacked babies in their cribs, children in their beds, helpless elderly people lost in dreams and reveries. En masse, they swarmed through back yards and parks, overcoming even the youngest and strongest. A million or more, they were an irresistible, bloodthirsty tide that could not be stopped or conquered. The rats fed upon the wealthy residents as if they were swift, buzzing flies and the people slow, dumb-witted cows ripe for slaughter.

* * *

Now unleashed, testing his prowess and the humans' mettle, contained in a form of amorphous energy in which Steven Russell was just a memory, Azarüb the all-powerful seethed and simmered in the middle of Pearl Harbor and gave the netherworld equivalent of a chuckle.

In the back of his mind, there was a pain: sharp, serious, persuasive.

Azarüb raged: Steven Russell's flame was still not quite extinguished.

It was the bitch, Azarüb knew. Her presence was giving Russell aid and comfort; otherwise, the human would have given up and died, allowed his consciousness to be entirely suffused in the demon's own. But no, the sow was making him hang on. And until Steven Russell utterly ceased to exist, Azarüb would never be entirely free. The human was a chancre, a bleeding sore, an ulcerous ache in the middle of Azarüb's being.

The bitch had to be destroyed.

Azarüb merely had *to think* and forces on the island would do his bidding.

And his bidding that night was that Marjorie Russell *die*.

CHAPTER ELEVEN

Honolulu

When the great explosion came, along with the wind and the dark clouds overhead, Kathy Bates had been doing a little night swimming in the well-lit outdoor pool of the Barrier Reef Hotel. The weather had been turning a little chilly, but that didn't bother her—she was still warm from the two or three drinks she'd consumed after dinner—and she swore her head was clear enough now and enough time had passed since eating for her not to worry about getting a cramp.

So she splashed about in the water in the middle of the luxurious courtyard and its overhanging balconies, surrounded by fancy, beautiful people and the rolling bars, cafés, canapés, and conversations that went with them. God, she was happy.

They had gone sight-seeing earlier in the day, Kathy and her two girlfriends, and this was the first opportunity she'd had to go into that large, lovely beckoning pool. Undeterred by the turn in the weather, a few other people had had the same idea. Kathy plunged right into the chlorine-ridden, aquamarine liquid and swam down, down to the bottom of the pool to touch it with her fingers.

She shot up out of the water. "Linda! Cecily! There's people down there!"

Linda and Cecily only laughed. They knew something she didn't.

"Silly!" Cecily said. "There's a bar underneath the pool. The bottom is transparent."

Kathy dove down again and realized they were telling her the truth; she hadn't been seeing things or suffering from a delayed variation of the D.T.s. There *were* people down there —she could see them through the transparent floor of the pool —and she supposed they could see her, too. She held her breath and peered down into the warm oak-and-gold room with its long polished bar, round tables filled to capacity, a man playing guitar in the corner. When someone at the bar looked straight up toward the ceiling and noticed her hanging there above him—their eyes met, *weird!*–she got all freaked out and rushed up to the surface of the water.

"That's *strange!*" she told her friends. "The people down there can look right up into the pool!"

She was wondering what would happen if there were ever a crack in the solid-glass bottom of the pool, when the *boom* came—everything seemed to *tilt* for a second—and then it was over and everyone around the pool, in the restaurant nearby, and probably down in the bar below, was talking all at once.

"What was that?"

"An explosion?"

"A sonic boom!"

"A plane?"

"Earthquake!"

After a while they talked in lower voices, but many still trembled and felt strangely frightened and disoriented for a long time after. Yet aside from a darkening of the sky, a little play of electricity in the clouds overhead, and a warm rush of a strong breeze over the hotel, nothing really seemed to have happened.

But there was a crack in the bottom of the pool.

After the boom, Pearl Harbor and the locales surrounding it, including Aiea and Honolulu, appeared to be in the eye of the storm—the weather was calmer; there were no high winds or lightning storms, as on the rest of the island.

But that didn't mean the inhabitants were safe by any means.

Kathy shuddered involuntarily and prepared to get out of the water. If it should start to thunder and lightning, she wanted to be safe under a canopy when it happened.

The crack widened.

Kathy tread water at the edge of the pool. "Linda, hand me that towel. It's chilly. I want to wrap it around me the minute I get out of the water." A heavyset grandmother type with a skintight black bathing cap on remained in the water, determined not to let lightning, black clouds, or *boom* ruin her fun. There were also about five other people in the pool.

Linda got up out of her chair and brought Kathy the towel. "C'mon, girl. Get outta the water. I'll wrap it around you so you don't catch cold."

Linda waited while Kathy reached out of the water, preparing to haul herself up the metal rungs affixed to the side of the pool. She held the pale blue towel outstretched in her hands, ready to receive her friend's shivering body.

Linda and Kathy both heard a loud, snapping, *crinkling* sound.

Kathy had no time to get out of the water.

The next second, she, the old lady, the other swimmers, and several tons of crushing water poured down through the hole in the bottom of the pool to splash and splatter indiscriminately into the tavern below. Drinkers at the bar were soon drenched with water and sliced apart by tremendous pieces of sharp, heavy glass; the old woman was decapitated by a particularly large chunk. Kathy fell through the hole, struggling to hold on to what little air there was in her lungs, and crashed onto one of the round tables with such impact that it collapsed under her weight and the couple sitting at it were thrown to the floor.

Kathy couldn't move. Her back was broken. She looked up through the hole in the ceiling and saw Linda, still holding the outstretched towel, staring down at her. There were several inches of water on the floor of the bar, as well as sprawled bodies and *pieces* of bodies, and a lot of shattered, gore-stained glass. There was also a great deal of blood smeared on the walls, the bar, and the screaming, trembling patrons.

Kathy lay there and sobbed as if her whole universe had just come tumbling down around her.

Which, of course, it had.

*** * ***

Downtown Honolulu

As the warm wind raced through the downtown district of the city it excited passions, sick desires, drove the already agitated minds of the residents and night prowlers into a frenzy. All along, Azarüb's slow emergence had exacerbated the natural tensions and resentments of the people in the district. Now that Azarüb was free, his influence was stronger than ever.

Gangs ran wild in the streets, overturning cars and smashing shop windows. Looters piled past broken glass and carried away TV sets and cameras. In the topless bars of the area naked women were pulled down from their stages and gang-raped by the patrons, bitten and torn and thrown aside once they'd been used and humiliated. Well-dressed whites became the target not just of single muggers but of roving packs of islanders who robbed them, beat them, even raped them and bashed in their brains afterward. Guns and knives came out to slash and splatter. The district had always been a powder keg; violence had always been below the surface, ready to erupt as it often did—but the police had never seen a night like that one.

Many of the police pulled out their guns and just fired and fired at anything or anyone that moved, regardless of their activity. A hooker here. A transvestite there. Rich tourist there. The lines between guilty and innocent, victim and perpetrator, began to narrow in their minds. Everyone was causing trouble, everyone should die. They enjoyed it—it was like blasting the heads off ducks in a shooting gallery. And there was no one to police the police.

All that mattered was the gushing of blood; all that mattered was *chaos*, the giving in to each and every dark impulse without exception. There was no restraint any longer. Criminals, tourists, cops, hookers, bikers—all became a multi-headed animal with one goal in mind: to kill, to break down, to destroy and erase and savage.

Stabbing and battering at one another all the while, a great mob of hysterical people from the downtown area swarmed into the hotel regions to loot and riot. They tore through lobbies, raced upstairs to rape strangers, wrecked shops and bars and destroyed and looted everywhere. Dead bodies began to pile up in the streets and hotels and taverns. The infection spread from the rioters to those vacationing in the resorts, and soon husband was beating wife, brother was raping sister, children were thrown from top-story windows, and blood was spattering everywhere. People were trampled underfoot by the mob. A woman would be yanked away from her husband, who would first cry in protest, but would then join the others and start the festivities by raping and beating his wife himself. The whole fabric of civilization was being torn asunder within the space of minutes. There was no way the unaffected could possibly have maintained order. It was a bloodbath.

But the dreadful events on the island were not limited to swarming rats, rioting humans, nature's storms out of control —there were other things, stranger things, happening. Phantoms and demons and creatures of the night were walking everywhere.

At the Tendai Mission of Hawaii, the statue of the Thousand-Armed Goddess of Mercy, Senju Kannon, nearly five times as tall as a man, ripped out of its foundation and walked, crushing cars and people underfoot, smashing walls of surrounding buildings, before falling to the ground and shattering into pieces.

In Diamond Head the rumbling continued as the floor of the crater grew white-hot. Any human who stayed there was boiled alive. A great bank of fiery smoke arose over the crater and any birds that remained in the area were broiled to ashes in an instant. The ranks of the National Guard headquartered at Diamond Head were decimated by the heat and steam. Survivors stood at the edge of the crater, gaping, and some of them swore they could hear the sound of the goddess Pele's laughter coming out of the fog.

* * *

In the Aiea Hills, where Timothy's house was located, it began quietly enough.

Frank, the diver, had sat down on a chair and requested a shot of whiskey. Marjorie had gone over to a corner and started weeping. Charles was stark white, drained of energy as well as color. Only Timothy remained in control. He turned on the TV and radio, tried the telephone, but all he could pick up was static. "It's happened. It's actually happened. We don't even know what's going on on the island."

But he could make a good guess. He could hear the death screams in his mind, hear the rumbling from Diamond Head, swear he could even hear the rioters in Honolulu as they went about smashing and killing. All that the others could hear was an abrupt, unnatural silence. The peacocks had finally stopped screeching.

"What do we do now?" Charles asked. "What can we do?"

Timothy was the type who took strength from adversity, from challenge, even from hopelessness. "We keep looking in my books for the answer. That's all we can do. And we lock the windows and bar the doors. It's going to be crazy out there tonight." He lifted his fist and shook it in the air. "It's not over yet, Azarüb. Not by a long shot." He turned to the others. "We can *still* force him back where he belongs."

Frank drained his shot glass in one gulp and got up to his feet. "I take it you don't need no diver no more."

"Hardly. If the demon's loose—"

Marjorie turned to the others and screamed, "It means Steven is dead, doesn't it? Really dead. Oh, God!"

"No, Marjorie—stop! We can't be sure about that. The demon has certainly overtaken Steven's mind or it would not have been able to free itself to move into our dimension. But that doesn't mean that Steven isn't alive somewhere inside Azarüb's essence, that we can't bring him back once the demon is defeated."

Charles interjected, "What about Steven's body. Is it…?"

"Intact? Possibly. Everything depends on that, of course, or he will die if there's no body to return to. But it's entirely possible that for his own purposes Azarüb has not harmed Steven's human shell. Azarüb might be walking around in the body, inhabiting it, wearing it while he adjusts to this dimension. Or he might have transformed Steven's body into a form of energy, which he absorbed, energy that might be reverted to flesh and blood once the demon is defeated."

Timothy was blathering; everyone knew that. He couldn't possibly be certain about any of this, but that meant it was not entirely implausible that his hastily formulated theories *were* correct. As long as there was a chance. It seemed that Steven's fate and the planet's fate were inextricably linked; save one and the other was saved. Maybe Steven's consciousness, though subjugated, was still active, still capable of aiding them in their fight against Azarüb.

Frank started for the door with words to the effect that he was concerned about his family. Before the diver could cover the distance, however, Cracker padded up the stairs from the den and walked past him, with her head bent low to the floor as if she were on a sacred mission or seeking prey. Timothy was not comforted by the fact that she was advancing steadily on Marjorie. The animals had been back to normal, relatively speaking, for the past few hours, but until now Timothy hadn't seen or heard from any of them since the explosion. Cracker did not look as distant and lethargic as usual, but purposeful and determined. The closer she got to Marjorie, the more alarmed Timothy became.

"Marjorie!" he shouted. "Get away from the dog!"

Marjorie's head shot up. She started to rise from the chair even as the dog's snarls grew loud enough for her finally to hear. Before she could get away from Cracker, the Setter lunged forward and bit down savagely on her right hand. Marjorie screamed in panic and anguish.

Frank and Charles converged on the dog and screeching woman and tried to pull the animal away. There was a danger of doing worse damage to Marjorie's hand in yanking the dog's teeth off the appendage than in simply letting Cracker hold onto it the way the dog was doing. Extremely agitated, Timothy darted out of the room, down the stairs, and into the den.

Downstairs, Timothy ran over to a glass case on the wall and removed a rifle that had been a present from a friend who loved hunting and gave out guns to people whether they wanted them or not. Timothy was glad he'd kept the weapon. He opened the drawer of a bureau below the case and desperately searched for the box of ammunition amid the clutter. *There*—he pulled out the box, dumped a few bullets into his hand, and loaded the rifle as quickly as possible. Marjorie's screams were ringing in his ears and he felt terribly frightened and helpless.

He ran upstairs to find that Frank had his hands on the dog's snout and was trying to wrench the jaws apart, while Charles held Marjorie close to his body, as if trying to siphon off her pain and absorb it into himself. Marjorie saw the rifle and knew what Tim intended to do.

"No!" she said. "Don't! I'm all right. Don't shoot the dog, please. I'll be okay."

Timothy hesitated. He saw blood, Marjorie's blood, dripping out of the dog's snout along with ounces of thick, white saliva. The dog was foaming at the mouth as if she had rabies. *Azarüb had corrupted his pet.* It would break his heart to shoot the Setter, but it wasn't really Cracker anymore. God, he loved that animal, that distant, dispassionate, lazy, silly, irascible, wonderful beast—he loved her. But he couldn't stand by and watch while she chewed Marjorie's hand off.

"Give me the rifle," Frank said in a no-nonsense voice.

Timothy waited only a second before he complied. He was more grateful to have had the decision taken out of his hands than he could say. He looked at Frank and flashed him a silent thank-you. *Mahalo.*

Taking the gun, Frank held the barrel in his fists and repeatedly smashed it into the Setter's back. Swak! Swak! The dog did not even seem to notice. Frank hit the beast harder and harder but it had no effect. Finally he lifted the rifle straight up in one hand and butted Cracker on the snout and head with the blunt bottom of the weapon. Cracker only snarled louder, bit into the hand harder—the dog would not let go.

"You'll have to shoot her, Frank," Timothy said. He reached out his hands to take the gun back, but Frank pushed him aside.

"Let me do it, okay? It'll be easier."

"Her hand!" Charles hollered. "You might hit Marjorie's hand."

"No. I'm going to shoot the dog in the chest. The shock will make it let go."

Frank raised the rifle. Charles gave Marjorie a comforting squeeze. In spite of her agony, Marjorie still protested against the shooting. Timothy turned away quickly and covered his eyes.

Bam!

When he turned around, Cracker had let go of the hand. She had dropped to the ground and was whimpering, bleeding. A large hole with black edges had opened up in her side.

"She's in pain," Timothy said, sobbing. "Please, Frank—finish the job."

The dog looked across the room for her master, her eyes met Timothy's eyes and pleaded—in those last seconds she was Cracker again, his Cracker—and it was his good old dog that died when Frank's second shot rang out and blew off part of her head.

Sickened, Marjorie ran downstairs into the den. Charles stayed a moment to comfort Timothy, who was still crying. Frank looked over at the old man, tears in his own eyes. "Sorry, man—but you know there was nothing else we could do."

"Th-thanks, Frank—for doing it for me. I-I couldn't…"

"*Uakaumaha au,*" Frank said. *I am sorry.* Timothy gave in to his feelings and just wept.

* * *

Down in the den Marjorie was heading for the extra bathroom to bandage her hand when she heard someone calling her name.

"Marjorie...Marjorie..."

She opened a door in one wall and entered a small room where she found garden equipment and a birdcage on a tall, slender stand. Inside the cage was a very large, beautiful parrot with red and green plumage. This was the bird Tim had mentioned. He had said the parrot had been acting up and had to stay in seclusion during their visit. Marjorie forced her mind off the pain in her hand and the repellent activity upstairs and went over to the cage... There was something about the bird, She *tried* to pull away—she knew the puncture wounds on her arm needed bandages and disinfectant—but she couldn't leave the room, just couldn't leave the parrot. She came closer and closer, put her face near the bars, and smiled at the little creature inside.

"Marjorie, Marjorie," it cooed. *Come closer, Marjorie,* it seemed to say. *I want to kiss you...*

By the time Charles had come downstairs to see where she was, Marjorie had opened the cage and the bird had flown out of its confinement. The bird was bigger than Marjorie's head. It immediately swooped at her and dug its tiny clawed feet into her face, started to peck at her nose and eyes. *Let me kill you, Marjorie,* the bird seemed to squawk. *I want to eat you, Marjorie...*

Hearing the commotion, Charles wrenched open the door to the storeroom and burst into the room. He put his hands on the parrot, pulled it off Marjorie, and threw it against the wall. The bird tumbled to the floor, hopped around as if in confusion, then abruptly renewed the attack.

Charles shoved Marjorie out into the den and then turned back toward the animal. The bird nipped at his ears, drawing blood, clawed at his hair and neck, all the time screeching, and even managed to tear small strips of flesh from Charles's hands and arms. Driven to desperation by the merciless assault, Charles grabbed up a rake and began to fight back against the bird.

Marjorie stood in the doorway, biting down on her fingers, and Charles ordered her away. "Shut the door! Shut the door!" he screamed. Instead, Marjorie grabbed a shovel leaning against the wall by the door and joined the offensive.

Using the implements, Marjorie and Charles were able to keep the parrot—which kept up a steady stream of foul language and threats against Marjorie—away from them and up against one corner of the chamber. Charles would have liked to maneuver the bird back into its cage, but that didn't seem possible. One of them would be too vulnerable if either of them dropped his or her weapon. If only Tim or Frank would come downstairs, but they were probably seeing to the dog's remains and had no idea what was happening. Marjorie gave the bird a good whack with her shovel and it looked as if it might be totally disoriented. It fluttered for a moment or two, then collapsed onto the floor.

When Charles cautiously approached the bird and bent over to see if it was alive, gave it a poke with the rake, it suddenly swooped up off the floor and made directly for the startled man's eyes.

"Damm it!"

Charles yanked it away from his face and held the squawking, squirming parrot against the wall. But it was pecking at his fingers, drawing blood, much blood. He tried to bat it with the rake, but the implement was not in an advantageous position. "Marjorie," Charles said helplessly.

Marjorie lifted her shovel and gave the bird another whack, and then another, and another…

"Marjorie, I think that's—"

Another and another and another…

The parrot stopped moving, stopped squawking, until it was a smear of blood and feathers smashed against the wall; it slid slowly down onto the floor and lay there in a crushed, gruesome heap.

Marjorie dropped the shovel with a clatter and let Charles take her in his arms. "Everything's going crazy, Charles. I'm going crazy. Look what I did..."

They turned to leave the room and saw Timothy and Frank looking in on them. Charles gave Timothy a weary, regretful shrug. "The bird..."

Marjorie was full of apology. "I shouldn't have let it out of the cage. I don't know why I did. It's like something came over me..."

Tim nodded, "It's all right. I understand." He sighed and held onto the open door to steady himself. He looked so tired. "My cat disappeared a long time ago, but the schnauzer is still on the loose. He's not on his bed, where he usually is. He might have gone outdoors earlier, or he could be on the prowl inside. Be careful, everybody."

"Look, I don't got no pets," Frank said, "but I gotta get home to my family, as long as everything's quiet here."

Timothy nodded. "Yes, yes, of course. Thanks for your help, Frank. I mean it. *Mahalo nui loa.*"

"*Aole pilikia,*" Frank said. *No trouble.*

But for the second time that evening Frank was not fated to get away so easily. They had all moved away from the storage room and closed the door, when there came a shattering of glass from upstairs. Timothy swore. "Now what!" He started to ascend the staircase while Frank went over to the sliding-glass doors that led out into the garden. "There's something out there," he muttered.

Frank slid one door open and peered out into the night. "Funny, I could swear—"

From one side of the door a great grunting beast tore out of the darkness and clamped its mouth over Frank's outstretched hand.

Timothy was halfway up the stairs to the upper level when a large, thudding object tore down from above and knocked him back down into the den.

Frank screamed for help. Timothy was writhing underneath a huge, mottled animal with enormous tusks coming out of either side of its misshapen mouth.

Charles had gone over to help Frank when the other sliding-glass door caved in in a welter of shards and chips and a third snarling animal roared into the enclosure.

Marjorie backed up in terror, stumbled on a chair, and fell sprawling to the floor.

Timothy managed to slide out from under the heavy animal on top of him, but he was out of wind and nearly crushed. The beast must have weighed three hundred pounds. He knew what they were. Wild Hawaiian boars. Over three feet high at the shoulder, with heavy thighs, big bellies, long snouts with tusks, all covered with a coat of wiry fur. The little pig eyes were cold and glaring. They were crafty and ferocious animals that normally stayed up in the isolated areas, where they belonged. It was not surprising that on this mad night they would come crashing down into the populated areas.

Frank pulled his hand out of the first boar's mouth and he was missing half a finger. He bent over in pain and threw up.

Charles lifted a large wooden chair and batted the pig on the head with it.

The boar that crashed through the glass skidded across the slick floor of the den on its way toward Marjorie. Marjorie scrambled to her feet and tried to get out of its way.

Tim rushed past the boar that had been on top of him and made his way up the staircase again. The boar tried to follow but found it more difficult to go up than it had been to come down.

The first pig shrugged aside the broken pieces of the chair Charles had hit it with and tried to back his attacker into a corner. Charles darted around the slower-moving animal and ran out into the garden. "Marjorie! Frank! Come this way!"

There was no way Marjorie could get past the boar pursuing her and follow Charles into the garden. She yanked open the door into the room where the bird had been and raced inside. The boar reached her just as she slammed the door in its hideous face. *Crash.* The door splintered but held. *Crack.* The boar butted the door again and this time a whole top section fell onto Marjorie's feet. The smaller cracks below deepened and widened, and more niches, through which the beast glowered, began to form. A few more strikes and the boar would be inside with her.

In his hurry to save his friends, Timothy nearly fell down the stairs—but he had his rifle. He lifted it, aimed it, blew a large chunk out of the side of the boar at the bottom of the staircase. The confused, mesmerized animal turned tail and ran out into the garden, where the first beast had gone to chase Charles.

Frank pointed his mutilated hand in the direction of the animal trying to break down the door to the storeroom. "Tim—Marjorie!"

Timothy aimed, fired, blew a hole in the back of the boar, which bellowed and turned toward its attacker. Timothy danced up the first few steps of the staircase. He fired again. The boar was slower and more dim-witted than normal, probably because it was Azarüb's idea that it come here, not its own.

A third shot and the beast lay dead on the floor of the den.

"Charles! Where's Charles?" Timothy hollered.

"I'm here."

A weary, scraped, and bleeding Charles Emerall stepped over the broken glass and walked back into the den from the garden. "I eluded them," he said, gasping. "They ran back up into the mountains." He collapsed onto the only chair left standing. "What next, Timothy? What next?"

Marjorie stepped out from the storage room and joined the others. She saw that Frank was staring at the stump of his missing finger in horror. "We have to bandage our hands," she said blankly.

The four of them sat or stood very quietly, listening to the night, wondering what else was out there, what would happen next.

"This was all because of me, wasn't it?" Marjorie said, still wearing that blank expression. "Azarüb wants to kill me. And the rest of you just got caught in the middle..."

"What's going on?" Frank asked. "My finger, my...Everything you said is true, old man, ain't it?" He tried to hold back tears but he couldn't. What was left of his finger must have been killing him.

"*Listen,*" Charles said.

They listened. Frank stopped his crying and Marjorie stopped her whimpering and Timothy and Charles tried to stop gasping in air long enough to hear what was happening.

They heard voices, a dozen voices, a hundred voices, calling, screeching, out into the night, voices that were carried on the wind and sailed into the den to stab into their hearts and bring them fear that was totally unparalleled with anything they had ever experienced before.

"*Oh, my God,*" Timothy whispered.

They went upstairs, turned out the lights, and peered out the front window in the indoor living room.

They were coming. Islanders, tourists, holding weapons, holding tools, dozens upon dozens of maddened human beings, coming to Timothy's house, converging on Timothy's house from all nearby points on the island, from the valley, the shore, and the forest, from Aiea and Pearl City and the other developments in the hills, with one—and only one—purpose in mind.

Each one of those men and women walking toward the house, up from the city, down from the mountains, had only one word on his or her lips. Timothy and Frank and Charles and Marjorie could hear that word distinctly, even over the chattering of their teeth, the roar of the fluid racing through their bloodstreams.

"*Marjorie!*" the people cried. "*Marjorie, Marjorie, Marjorie...*"

CHAPTER TWELVE

"Let's get the fuck outta here!" Frank screamed. *"Wiki wiki!"*

There was a path through the woods—a shortcut—that Frank used to go from his house, farther up in the hills, to Timothy's. They went back down to the den—Timothy paused to grab two books from the study, much to Frank's annoyance —and went out into the garden. In a minute they had gone through a gate in the back, walked up an incline covered with orange hibiscus and multihued tulip trees, and were making their way through the woods toward Frank's *hale.*

From concealment they turned back to stare at Timothy's house.

Nearly a hundred people were tearing it apart, crashing through windows, gnashing their teeth and grunting, smashing everything they touched, shoving one another aside to be the first to find Marjorie, to tear her living heart from her breast. Marjorie seemed numb with terror. For the first time Timothy realized exactly what they were up against. They were helpless, it was hopeless. *He can turn the whole world against us.* If the information he needed wasn't in one of these two remaining volumes…

There was no time for Timothy to mourn his dog, his parrot, the destruction of his house, as the horde trampled everything in it to tatters, no time for anything but to keep Marjorie safe. In the darkness of the woods he took her hand and said, "Think of Steven, Marjorie. All the time, *think of Steven*. Let him know you love him! Let him know you're near! Help him fight Azarüb, Marjorie! Help him!"

Timothy took solace in the fact that so far they had survived Azarüb's various attacks—*they had survived*—which meant that the demon was not yet all-powerful, and in spite of the death and destruction on the island there was a chance to defeat him. Marjorie was the key. Marjorie and Steven and their love for each other.

Marjorie could not necessarily blame herself for what happened at his house. Timothy presented at least as much of a danger to Azarüb, and though he tried to keep up his psychic defenses and shield his whereabouts from the demon's probes, he knew Azarüb had certainly become aware of his existence when Timothy's mind linked with Steven's on the memorial.

They arrived at Frank's place in fifteen minutes. They could still hear the mob back at Timothy's chanting *Marjorie, Marjorie, Marjorie*, an insane chilling litany.

Frank's wife and two children were all right, but scared.

"What's happening?" Amiko asked. She took them inside and washed and bandaged all their injuries, most of which had been sustained on their hands. An anxious, nervous Frank told her a story about a crazy mob and wild boars, but nothing about Steven Russell or demons.

Hurry, hurry, Timothy kept thinking, as Marjorie's hand was wrapped in gauze and treated with disinfectant. *Wiki wiki*. The trouble with Marjorie maintaining, strengthening, her link with Steven was that the demon knew what Steven did—assuming Steven's consciousness still existed at all—and would know where Marjorie was. The only chance they had was to keep one step ahead of Azarüb's minions. They had to go someplace so isolated that no one could reach them until he had time to stop and read his books or formulate *some* plan…

"Frank," Timothy said, "you have a hunting lodge in the Waianae mountains, don't you?"

"Yes." He was still in shock over losing half the finger. Amiko, a former nurse, wrapped a tourniquet around his wrist, but the hand would need medical attention if and when this insanity was over.

Timothy indicated himself and Charles and Marjorie. "Could we go there tonight? The three of us? *Now?* These people"—he referred to the mob they'd narrowly escaped—"they'll learn where Marjorie is sooner or later. For your family's sake, we should leave immediately."

Amiko looked utterly perplexed but said nothing. Timothy could only imagine what was going through her mind. She probably thought they were fugitives from justice running from a lynch mob—headed by wild boars! He would have laughed had the situation not been so critical.

After what he'd been through that evening, Frank did not need any persuading. He gave Timothy hurried directions and the keys. "Take my car," he said. "I've got my motorcycle here in case of emergencies. Good thing I walked to your place tonight, huh?"

"You're a good man, Frank. A good *aikane*." *Friend.*

Frank's eyes were teary again. "I'm scared, man, really scared." He took Timothy aside and whispered, "What do I do to protect my family? Will we go berserk like those others did?"

"I hope not," Timothy said, wanting to reassure him but unable to do so completely. "The demon exaggerates weakness and vulnerability—evil, you might say—in the human soul. You and your family are good, strong people and may be able to resist. Those people who attacked us have probably been affected in some manner for a long time now; it doesn't happen overnight. Just stay indoors—don't go out for anything. Once we're gone the demon won't be concerned with you. We'll be out of your reach, out of everyone's. Stay inside—and let's hope everything works out."

How could he tell the man, his wife, his two little *keikis*, that it may have been the end of the world? Better to put a gun to one's head and die in one's own time and fashion than have to suffer death at the hands of Azarüb or one of his slaves.

They had to leave immediately. Timothy thought he could hear the chanting voices coming closer. It was only a matter of time before the existence of the shortcut to Frank's place was picked out of Marjorie's or Timothy's mind by Steven—and, hence, the demon—and communicated to the howling mob. It was only their shuffling lack of free will and organization that prevented them from getting there already.

As Timothy and Charles and Marjorie drove away from Frank's *hale*—on a road that went nowhere near Timothy's house—a snarling, furry animal jumped at the automobile in an attempt to attack Marjorie. There was a thud, a bump, and the creature smacked off the hood and was crunched underneath the car's wheels.

The whole world is going crazy.

Timothy had caught only a glimpse of the dead animal, but a glimpse had been enough. He said nothing to his friends.

The dead animal had been Simon, his schnauzer.

Azarüb, he swore, I will make you pay.

* * *

Compared to what they had been through already, the trip to the Waianae mountains was uneventful. They stayed on back roads and skirted populated areas whenever possible. They dodged a few more wild boars in the road, there were cracks in the windshield from the occasional attacking hawk or bat, but Timothy sensed these incidents had less to do with Marjorie than with the general lunacy on Oahu. He was relieved to see that the wrath of the storm had lessened and the skies even seemed to be clearing, though if that had to do with their location or something else he couldn't say. For a while they'd driven through a real downpour—the wind had been so fierce he'd had trouble keeping the car on the road—but the closer it got to morning the nicer the weather became. Even Azarüb couldn't keep it up forever, he supposed. Even demons had to rest, conserve their energy. Demons loved the night. *But*, he reminded himself, *demons could also be tricksters.*

Frank's cabin was small but serviceable and they found it easily. It was at the end of a narrow road in a clearing surrounded by a forest of flowering jacarandas and golden shower trees. Marjorie's hand was aching—she took some aspirin that had been left in the bathroom. The only good thing about the pain was that it probably took her mind off everything else. There was a little food in the cupboard— canned goods and packages—and Timothy instructed Charles to make them an early breakfast while he read. The two volumes he'd grabbed from his library were the only other major possibilities he could think of...

Besides, reading would take his mind off the disturbing fact that his world, the whole world itself, was going crazy. Neighbors, friends, probably other people he knew, attacking, wrecking his house mindlessly at the direction of some nether-god. *He shuddered to think of himself and the others at the mercy of that crowd, being torn apart...*It was a wonder Charles and Marjorie, especially Marjorie, were bearing up as well as they were. Azarüb, the alien, had turned the three of them into aliens, too, strangers in an awful forbidden land. In this land they were germs, and the islanders, antibodies, sent to destroy them.

Don't think about it, don't think! his mind screamed. *Just read. Read!*

Marjorie wasn't hungry. She excused herself and went into the next room to lie down.

An hour later Timothy, still hunched over his books, cried out excitedly, then went over to shake Charles awake from where he'd fallen asleep in a rocking chair. "Get Marjorie," he said.

Charles came back from the other room a moment later by himself.

"Still sleeping?" Timothy asked.

Charles shook his head. "She's gone."

They heard the car starting outside. She must have climbed through the window...the fool...what did she think she could do?

Tim and Charles ran out into the narrow lane outside the cabin...

...to see the taillights of Frank's car receding into the distance and disappearing altogether when Marjorie turned a bend in the road...

I'm coming, Steven. I'm coming. Hold on, darling, I'm coming.

Marjorie had fallen asleep in the bedroom. Finally. A deep sleep. But in spite of that, she still had dreams. Dreams of Steven.

The dreams did not take place in that awful ship this time; there were no bleeding walls, no skeletons, no dark sinister creatures or giant hands. Only Steven. He was awash in a yellow ring like the corona of the sun and he was smiling. "I've won," he told Marjorie. "It's over." Steven looked so young and handsome, just as he had when they were married. She cried in her sleep, delirious with happiness. *If only this were true, if only...*

When she woke up she could still hear Steven's voice—and she knew what she had to do. Steven was telling her that Azarüb had been defeated, sent back to his horrible world, and Steven was free and whole again. For proof all she had to do was look out the window and see how completely clear the sky was. She looked. And Steven was right. It was nearly dawn and there wasn't a cloud in the sky. She could see the fading, sinking moon, the distant, vanishing stars, felt a sense of happiness and peace. *Steven was saved.*

But she also knew—somehow—that Steven did not want her to tell Charles or Timothy just yet. Well, she was sure that they could see the skies for themselves, that Timothy with his extrasensory powers or whatever would *know* that things were all right now. She had done what Timothy said—kept thinking of, bolstering, Steven—and it had *worked.* Everything was all right again, the world was safe. Her brave, wonderful Steven had vanquished the dragon, sent the monster back where it belonged.

Neither she nor Steven wanted anyone else to witness this reunion. They wanted to be all alone when they were finally reunited after forty years. She knew the men would understand. She felt some slight doubt, a nagging anxiety, underneath her elation, but she thought it best to ignore it. What could be wrong now that Steven was okay?

So she sneaked out through the window. Luckily, Timothy in his haste and confusion had left the keys in the car. Now she was driving through the mountains, not sure of her destination, but letting Steven steer her all the while. It was in her head, that was all—the right way to go, the right turn to take at a crossroads, it was instinctive. Soon, *soon,* she and Steven would be together again. Look—the sun was starting to come up, day was breaking. Everything was all right. Somehow —*somehow*—Steven had won. *Steven had won!*

Marjorie was so thrilled at the prospect of seeing her beloved again that she continued to ignore that nagging apprehension in the back of her mind, the doubt, the guilt over running off the way she had without telling anyone, taking the car. She thought nothing of what it would mean to have Steven back in the world of the 1980s after his being entombed for forty years. Nothing mattered but getting to the spot where Steven was waiting for her.

Her journey took her down from the mountains and toward the shore, through tunnels cut right into solid rock with bushy green coiffures of plants and trees. She passed acres of green fields, deserted lava headlands, and coves and beaches cut into the hills above the shore. Although she was now driving along a precarious cliffside highway, she felt as if God Himself were guiding and protecting her with each rotation of the axle. She took each swerve, each turn, as if possessed. She who hadn't driven in years barreled over the roads as if she were a tour guide who knew each curve by heart. She never thought of the possible danger, only of her destination and the person who was waiting for her.

She was surprised that Steven would not wait for her at Pearl Harbor, near the ship. For she sensed that her drive was taking her to another part of the island altogether. An isolated part of the island, where there were no cars, people, or naval installations, no police or John Q. Citizens to interfere; a romantic rendezvous where they could be alone, fully alone.

She drove.

* * *

The white force shaped like an anthropomorphic bullet sped through the water from Pearl Harbor, past Ford Island, up the northern coast of Oahu, barreling through the ocean like a torpedo, moving at incalculable speed, zooming, zooming, toward the tiny inlet, the hidden cove, about two-thirds of the way up the shore.

The bullet streaked through the waves and headed for the small beach hidden amid the pandanus trees and coconut palms. A multitude of small fish and crustaceans darted out of its way.

When the bullet emerged from the ocean it had taken the form of a man.

One particular man. One special man.

The man, naked, rested on the sand for a moment, taking stock of himself, how he felt, how best to deal with the situa-

tion. Part of his mind was very active, directing someone to this very site, someone who would arrive in only a few moments.

The man saw a path leading up to a hill overlooking the ocean. A steep path. A high hill. The road, he sensed, was not far from the cliffs edge. She would be coming along that road.

The man started up the path.

* * *

"Now what do we do?" Charles was ranting. "We're stuck on this mountain without a car. And Marjorie is driving off to God knows where and will probably get herself killed."

Timothy was standing silently over near the cabin's front window. "I know where she's going," he said finally, "and why. The telepathic emanations she's responding to are so strong that I discovered I can pick them up, also. She thinks she's going to Steven. She looked at the clear sky and thought that Steven had won."

Charles blanched. "You mean it *isn't* over. My God—we've got to go after her!"

"I know how to stop Azarüb," Timothy stated.

Charles rushed over to his friend's side. "Then do it, Tim, do it! Before it's too late!"

Timothy looked terrible; his old eyes were hollow and his face long and gray. "I have...I have to be in the demon's presence," he said.

"Good Lord! Are you sure? Are you sure you've found the answer?"

Timothy tapped the large, dusty, dilapidated book he had been perusing before Marjorie's disappearance. "As sure as I can be from reading something in one of these ancient manuscripts." He *hoped* the book was correct. If not...*if not, everything would be lost.*

Charles was a study in barely restrained hysteria. "But

how do we get to Azarüb? We don't know where he is—or what he is—now that he's left the ship!"

Timothy put a calming hand on Charles's shoulder for a moment, patted him gently, but said nothing. Then he started forward, stopped abruptly a few seconds later, then continued moving again toward the back of the cabin. Confused, Charles followed him down the hall until they reached the back door. Timothy explained as they went out into the yard. "Frank mentioned something about a truck he keeps here that he used to bring old furniture up from his house to the cabin. If it's still here…"

It was. Sitting among rusted chairs, discarded tires, broken bureaus, and piles of newspaper. A battered old pickup truck that looked as if it were about ready to collapse and probably would if they turned on the engine.

The two men could have kissed it.

There was a problem, however. The keys were not in the ignition. Back indoors, Timothy and Charles searched frantically in every drawer and cupboard they could find, hoping Frank had secreted the keys to the vehicle somewhere inside the cabin.

"I found them," Charles said. "At least I hope it's them!" The keys, along with several other items, were in a coffee can that was next to a jar of moldy peanut butter and some solidified packaged rice.

They ran outside. As Charles warmed up the truck—which coughed, guffawed, belched, and shuddered, but finally started—Timothy looked in a shed and found a can of stored gasoline. He put it in the back of the pickup. Then he went into the house and came out carrying his book and a few smaller items, shoving them into his pockets as he went. He climbed up into the cab with a groan. "Let's go," he said.

The sun was starting to come up and the sky was a striking shade of deep purple. The air smelled fresh with that lovely island aroma.

"Are you sure it isn't over?" Charles asked. "It's so peaceful, so beautiful."

"Peace and beauty can be deceptive," Tim said.

The truck drove along the narrow lane beside the cabin and turned onto the road that led down off the mountain toward the shore.

* * *

Marjorie knew she was almost there. Her foot pressed down on the gas pedal. Hurry, hurry. *She was almost there.* Her heart was beating fast and her breath was quickening. *Almost there, almost there,* she said to herself over and over again.

She went around what she knew was the final curve in the winding road and she *was* there; the place she was supposed to be. The side of the road facing the cliff widened out into a grassy slope that rose high, high above the level of the highway. At the bottom of this hill, leading down from the road, there was a steep path through some bushes that led down to one of the prettiest coves she had ever seen. She parked the car at the bottom of the hill on the grass, then stepped out. She was sure Steven was waiting for her down there in that lovely little lagoon. It was perfect. She was so excited, so ecstatic, nothing would have stopped her from descending, nothing but...

"*Marjorie.*"

She turned. Steven was not down in the cove, he was on top of the hill! Partially hidden by the tall grass and weeds, he had been bending down by the edge of the cliff. He stepped forward. He was totally naked but it did not strike Marjorie as odd; after all, everything about this situation was odd—oddly wonderful. He had cheated death, defeated a demon, broken all the rules—what was mere nakedness up against that? She was struck by how beautiful he was, how young and beautiful. The fine limbs, flat stomach, the strong, swimmer's build.

And so handsome. He looked not one day older than when she had last seen him over forty years ago. If anything, he was more perfect than she remembered.

"*Marjorie.*"

Steven started coming down the hill toward her. She tried to move, to run toward him, but she couldn't take a step, she couldn't even breathe, she was so overwhelmed by the moment. She could only stand there by the car, breathing in, breathing out, quivering, sobbing so much she could barely see through her tears, overcome by a million emotions. *This was the man she loved, the man she had held in her heart for over forty years, the man she had thought of every hour, day after day, every minute since the last time she'd seen him. This was the man whose life she had shared even after his death, the man she had communicated with, slept with, every night of her life; the man who walked beside her with every step she took; who inhaled along with her every last breath she breathed.* The man she loved more than anything else in the world.

"Steven, *Steven...*"

As he reached the bottom of the slope, she finally broke free of her trance, her trauma, the blessed inertia of her all-encompassing fantasy-come-real, and ran pell-mell into his arms. She held onto him, clutched his body inside her own, kissed him and hugged him and crushed him against herself as if wanting to envelop his life force, to absorb and nurture every little part of him—every cell, every thought, every feature—and keep him from ever leaving her again.

"Steven, I love you!" she cried. "I love you. I love you. *Oh, Steven.*"

As she sobbed in his arms, her husband's face took on a shimmer, an unholy radiance, and the lips pulled back in an expression of loathing and contempt.

CHAPTER THIRTEEN

Sometime before Marjorie was at last reunited with her husband, Timothy and Charles were careening down a coast highway toward the spot where the uncanny rendezvous was taking place. The emanations from the brain of "Steven" were still quite strong, still guiding Marjorie, and Timothy had no trouble picking up those emanations and following the same winding path that Marjorie did. Azarüb had senses far beyond those of human beings; senses with which the demon was able to discern the layout of the Oahu terrain, determine the best spot for his emergence from the sea, and the perfect place to destroy Marjorie once and for all. That way he would utterly crush her chances of inspiring what was left of Steven's consciousness to rebellion.

Timothy had an advantage over Marjorie in that he knew the length and breadth of Oahu, had driven across it and over the mountains and along the shore many times. He knew many of the secret coves and lagoons that were popular with the natives, undiscovered by tourists, spots that would be completely deserted at this hour of the morning. He knew what Marjorie's destination was even before she did. Sensing that Marjorie's rusty driving ability was not meant for narrow byways and bumpy side roads, the demon guided her along the comparatively safe, paved, if exotic highways. Timothy, in his old but sturdy truck, had no such disadvantage. Therefore, he arrived at the cove where she and Steven were reunited only moments after Marjorie did.

The sun had not yet risen completely, but its light was penetrating the dark sweep of the departing evening—the world was now bathed in a bluish-gray glow that was similar to twilight. The witching hour was long since over, but not the danger they were in. What they faced was far worse than any witch or sorcerer. What they faced wasn't even human.

Now to convince Marjorie of that.

Timothy parked the truck next to Frank's car and he and Charles burst out of the cab. They were not too late. Marjorie and a naked young man—*Steven*—were walking arm in arm up the slope away from the road. They were already halfway toward the cliff. They seemed not to have noticed the men's arrival.

"Marjorie!" Charles cried.

"Steven" was the first to turn and look back at the two men on the road. His expression was blank, the brow furrowed, as if the beast were trying to figure out what its correct response —and therefore facial attitude—should be. Marjorie turned around a moment later and her eyes widened, though whether she was glad or annoyed to see them was not readily apparent. She stopped, then tried to pull away from Steven and move down the hill.

"Charles! Timothy!"

Steven's hand held tightly onto Marjorie's, however, and with a gentle yank she was pulled back to his side. Apparently Steven wanted to continue walking up the hill.

"Darling, it's the men who *helped* you," she said, smiling brightly. "I want you to meet them! You must meet them! Come on!"

Steven bent his head and whispered into Marjorie's ear. Timothy wished he could hear what he was saying.

When Steven was through, Marjorie pinched his cheek and said merrily, "Silly, we can spend *all day* together afterward! I just want you to say hello and then we'll do whatever you want, dear."

She tried again to pull away from Steven, but he only held on tighter, jerking her back to his side as if she were a Yo-yo. She did not seem to sense anything amiss, however; she only thought he was exhibiting a possessiveness that she clearly found totally charming.

"Fellows!" she yelled to Timothy and Charles, who were already making their way up the slope. "Come here and say hello to Steven. He's a bit bashful—understandably. Maybe you can lend him some clothes. Isn't it wonderful? I have him back, can you believe it? I have him back, and I have both of you to thank."

Marjorie was in immediate danger. Although there was something that Timothy would have liked to have gotten out of the body of the pickup, he was afraid to take the time. She and Steven were much too close to the cliff! Besides, it might take the strength of both men if they were to stop Steven from suddenly grabbing up Marjorie and hurling her off the edge. They were two frail old fellows and Steven was young and powerful. Even if the demon's powers were limited while he took human form—which may not have been the case—he would still be more than a match for two doddering senior citizens.

There were only a few feet between the two men and Marjorie now. Steven held on tightly to Marjorie, one arm around the waist, his other arm entangled with Marjorie's, but it looked more and more like an armlock instead of an embrace. Marjorie, blinded by adoration, didn't sense that she was slowly being dragged to the edge of the cliff, didn't sense anything but what she'd nursed and fabricated in her own mind during forty years' time. Timothy was struck by how grotesque a pair the two of them made: the physical differences, the age difference, the young slender boy, and the chunky, wrinkled widow behaving absurdly as if she were a young girl... She should have been glad it was *not* Steven, not the cruel ironic jest it appeared to be. Couldn't she see for herself...? He wanted to feel pity for her, but there was so much at stake!

"Listen to me, Marjorie!" Timothy said, holding out his arms imploringly. "Listen. That...that man who's holding you is not Steven. It's *not Steven*, Marjorie! That thing holding you is *Azarüb* in human form. He has stolen Steven's body, stolen his identity—"

Marjorie shrieked in outrage and denial and refused to listen. "*No. No!* Why are you saying that? This *is* Steven. Can't you see that? My Steven. You two have never even met him. Don't you think I would know my own husband—"

"Just because the sky has cleared doesn't mean that the evil is over or that Azarüb has been defeated," Timothy insisted. "I can still sense the demon's presence, and I tell you, Marjorie—*that is not your husband!* It *isn't!* Azarüb is trying to trick you. He wants to destroy you, destroy every shred of Steven's consciousness left inside of him. Believe me, woman, *that is not your husband!*"

"No! *No!*" She looked protectively at Steven. He had managed to put on a perplexed, hurt expression that was so realistic that Timothy found himself actually admiring his adversary. *Then Steven looked straight at Timothy and the old man felt himself nearly freeze to the spot with terror.*

Steven turned back to Marjorie. "Who are these guys?" he asked in a voice that was so young and innocent it was positively shocking. "What are they talking about?"

Charles stepped forward in a sudden thrust. "There, *there,* you see!" he said to Marjorie. "If that is Steven, then how can he *not* know what we're talking about, when he was Azarüb's prisoner for forty years? Answer me, demon, answer me! And why is he so young, hmm? He *should* be in his sixties, like you and *me.* Answer me that, demon!"

A shimmer of dismay or panic flew across Steven's face. Then he quickly reestablished facial control and said, "I'm not Azarüb, I tell you!" His voice became high and whiny and it looked as if he might burst into tears. "I'm just so *confused,* that's all. I was down there in that ship for so *long...*"

He stood up tall and straight like a good soldier and insisted, "I'm not Azarüb! They're crazy, Marjorie. I won, I tell you, *I won!* I defeated the demon, sent it right back where it came from. I was the one who conjured it in the first place." He rattled his head. "Boy, was I ever stupid!"

Azarüb was doing a wonderful job of mimicking Steven's voice and gestures, Timothy knew, but there was something about the performance that nevertheless stamped it as play-acting. Had Marjorie not been so enraptured, she might have noticed it. But this was a man she had not seen since 1941, after all. No matter how much she loved him or doted on his memory, she couldn't be expected to remember everything about him, especially not exactly as it was. It was *this* that the demon was counting on. It knew the words, it had the right memories—it could pick them out of her and Steven's minds. But Azarüb still wasn't Steven Russell. Sooner or later he would make a mistake—*but meanwhile he was gently, gently, moving Marjorie farther up the hill, closer and closer to the edge of the cliff...*

Marjorie continued to squeal her denials, while Steven protested his innocence. In other circumstances Timothy might have appreciated the bizarreness of the situation. Any moment now the demon would be close enough to the edge to kill Marjorie, to smash her down upon the rocks and surf below, and nothing would matter. They might still defeat the beast, but it would be too late to save the woman. Timothy was determined not to let that happen.

It was a gamble but they had no choice. He decided to tell Charles that their only chance now was to rush Steven and pull Marjorie away from him before the two of them got any closer to the cliff. But before he could whisper anything to his comrade, the demon used its unique telepathic link with Marjorie—its ability to snatch dreams and hopes and fears out of all human minds—to create more time-consuming mischief. Something passed between "Steven" and his wife that did not require vocalization. Marjorie's eyes grew cold and angry and she literally spat in Charles's direction.

"I know why you're doing this!" she screamed at him. "You're jealous, *jealous*—you want to take me away from Steven. Steven told me—he told me all about you. My husband was a *hero*, he died fighting for his country"—she indicated Timothy with a sneer—"even this silly old man volunteered for service during World War Two. But you didn't fight, you wouldn't fight, because you were German-American and your whole family was against the war. They wouldn't *let* you fight, you wouldn't fight—you coward, you *Nazi*—and you were put in a camp in Arizona for the duration of the war."

Timothy could tell from the look on Charles's face that it was true.

"Emerall isn't even your real name, is it? It's Gunter Voss, isn't it? That's why you never talk about what you did during the war, while my Steven was *dying*. You changed your name after they let you out of the camp. And later on you married a Jew, your Clara, and years later, when Clara found out about where you'd been during the war, how you turned your back on your adopted country and refused to fight the Germans, the Jew-hating *Nazis*, she hated you, didn't she? *Hated you.* Hated you for your neglect, your cowardice, your betrayal, and your hypocrisy. And after she killed herself, do you know what her spirit said to you through that medium you went to?

You lied when you told me her message wasn't clear. It was very clear—she told you how much she *loathed* you…"

In all the years Timothy had known his younger friend, he'd never known this about him. He was not shocked; it had all happened long ago. Gunter-Charles had obviously been born in Germany, come over to America in his early adulthood, and, in all good conscience, couldn't bring himself to fight against his former countrymen. He had paid for that decision with internment during the war. He was no Nazi, Timothy knew that. But Marjorie, fueled by the demon's subtle mental maneuvering, was not about to forgive Charles anything.

"Please, Marjorie," Charles said, his shoulders drooping in despair and mortification. "Please, that was so long ago…"

Timothy had a plan. Marjorie was near the breaking point. He *had* to get her away from Steven. They were drawing closer and closer to the cliff… If he managed to get her angry enough…

"Talk about hypocrisy!" Timothy said, mustering as much vocal contempt as he could manage. "Your 'Steven' is no hero. This little boy, this child—this is what you call a 'hero'? He was such a coward—so afraid of what might happen to him— that he conspired with an evil demon just to save his own life. He's a *coward*, a—"

Marjorie's eyes flared with rage. "Stop that, you miserable old man! He couldn't have known what would happen… He wanted to *live* so he could return to me and my baby!"

Timothy snorted. "Wake up, Marjorie! A young good-looking man like that! You think he cared about you or your baby? He probably couldn't wait to get rid of you. You trapped him into marriage using the oldest trick in the book, bitch—you got pregnant. And there he was, twenty-one, and saddled with an ugly pregnant wife he probably only slept with to get his rocks off. You honestly think you would have held on to him—that irresponsible, self-centered, cowardly *asshole*—do you honestly think you'll hold on to him now?"

That did it. Enraged, screeching, Marjorie tore away from Steven so quickly the man hadn't a chance to snatch her back. She quickly skirted the short distance between herself and Timothy and threw herself at the older man, beating at him with upraised fists, shoving him so hard that he toppled to the ground.

"Charles!" Timothy shouted through Marjorie's onslaught. *"Now.* Attack him, beat him, anything—if we can defeat him while he's *human…"* There was a chance, still a chance, and then Timothy would not have to resort to the terrible ultimate act he might have to perform to stop Azarüb.

Charles bent down and picked up a large, heavy rock in his hand. He stepped toward Steven, who seemed disoriented, and swung it at the young man's face. Steven backed up.

Marjorie had Timothy on the ground. She seemed to be beginning to realize how she was behaving; her assault diminished and she stared at her fallen adversary in shock and dismay. But her tears and anger remained.

To keep her occupied, to prevent her from helping "Steven," Timothy slapped her viciously across the face. "Bitch!" he cried.

She literally snarled at him and tried to scratch out his eyes. For an old woman she was a hellcat. The two of them began to roll back and forth on the grass, trying to dodge each other's blows, screeching and hollering and tearing at each other. Timothy was afraid he had let it go too far, but he'd had no other option.

Near the cliff edge, Charles and Steven were still engaged in battle. The demon did not seem to know how to fight while wearing this human form. Azarüb had absorbed Steven's memories, true, but Steven had never been much of a fighter, first of all, and the demon had not yet had a chance to become acclimated enough to the body to know how to use it. Azarüb didn't know the moves. Charles got in close enough to bash the younger man on the head with the rock. He was appalled —*what if Timothy was wrong about this and he was trying to kill an actual, living person?*—but he moved in quickly for a second strike. A punch from Steven chanced to graze his chin and he fell back. He almost lost his grip on the rock. Charles prayed the demon would not revert to his natural form—then Azarüb might have all his power back and could sweep him out of existence with a thought.

Timothy had managed to swivel on the ground at such an angle that he and Marjorie, still entangled, rolled over and over and began tumbling down the hill. With the sky overhead and grass below, Marjorie's snarling, dripping face became a nauseating blur as they sped down toward the road in one circular motion after another. When they came to a messy, painful halt by the roadway, Timothy was on top and hence the first to recover. Heavier, bulkier, Marjorie couldn't move as fast, and she seemed very dazed and dizzy. A spot of blood on her temple indicated that she had hit her head on a rock by the road. Pulling something out of his pocket, Timothy ignored the woman for the moment and raced back up the hill as fast as he could go.

At the very edge of the cliff, practically dangling high above the pounding waves and jagged outcroppings, Steven and Charles were furiously writhing for dominance. Charles was more ferocious, the better fighter, but Steven was younger. Even a glancing blow from Steven did Charles harm, while the rain of punches he hurled at the younger man appeared to do comparatively little damage. Yet both of them were bruised, black and blue, bleeding from numerous scrapes and injuries. Timothy held his breath—Charles had slipped on a patch of dirt dangerously close to the edge. He tottered for a moment on his heels, swung precariously over the precipice, then flung himself down onto the ground, where he lay hugging the earth and gasping.

Steven lifted the rock Charles had dropped and raised it high above his head.

Timothy held out the knife he had taken from Frank's cabin—a long, sharp butcher knife—and rammed it into the side of the young man's stomach.

The rock dropped, missed Charles's head, fell off the edge, and plunged into the ocean.

Steven's eyes flew open in shock.

Timothy pulled the knife out, rammed it in again. And again.

Marjorie, rushing up the hill, roared and bellowed.

Timothy thrust the knife in again. *Again.*

Blood dripped out from Steven's torso and spattered onto Charles's face like crimson raindrops as he pulled himself up from the ground.

As Steven began to topple, fall to the grass, Timothy lifted the knife and slit the man's throat.

Moments after Steven hit the ground he was dead.

Marjorie was too shattered, too weary, to scream. Tears ran down her face and she sank to her knees over Steven's body. "Murderers. Murderers." She hadn't the energy to pronounce the damning words above a whisper. *"Murderers."* Unmindful of the blood, she cradled her husband's head in her hands and kissed him. "Why did you have to kill him? *Murderers!"*

Charles was horrified. The dead man didn't look like a demon; he looked like a man.

"What have we done, Timothy?" he asked. "What have we done?"

For a moment Timothy himself was full of doubt. No—he couldn't have made a mistake. The evil had still been so strong, so pervasive.

"According to legend, if you kill a demon while it is in human form, the demon dies," Timothy said.

"Shouldn't it revert to its demonic form?" Charles asked.

"It...it should. Perhaps in a moment..."

Marjorie threw herself across her beloved's body, screeching in torment, hollering her loss for the world to hear, tearing at her hair, beating her breast. The exhibition cut into Timothy's soul worse than any knife blade. He felt for a pulse, but there was none. *He'd slit his throat, stabbed his heart—the man was dead.* But how could it be, *how could it have happened...?*

"Good God—I've killed a man."

Steven's eyes flew open.

"No, *you haven't,*" Steven said.

* * *

Marjorie gasped.

Steven threw her to one side and began to rise to his feet. As he ascended, the knife wounds, including the gory gash in his throat, began to heal themselves. It looked like frames of a film running in reverse, slashes disappearing, mending, blood dripping backward.

Charles gulped. "Oh, my God."

By the time Steven was standing on two feet, there wasn't a single injury—not a mark—on his body.

"Charles!" Timothy screamed. "Keep him occupied. It didn't work. I have to run down to the truck!"

Marjorie wailed, "*Steven!*"

Just for an instant "Steven" looked down at his wife. "Shut up, you pig!"

"*Steven!*"

Charles lifted a trembling hand in warning. "Marjorie—get away from him, *please!*"

Marjorie looked helplessly at Charles. The jubilation of the moment—Steven's coming back from the grave a second time —had been dissipated, turned to bitter dross, all in an instant. Charles could tell that she knew it wasn't Steven. She knew they had been right all along.

"Steven! Oh, my God, no—*Steven!*"

Steven's countenance was leering and hideous, though the outward features had not changed. The voice was darker and deeper. The eyes glowed with a scorching maleficence.

"Marjorie, get away from him—quickly!"

Steven made a grab for the woman, but she managed to get to her feet and run away before he could reach her. He swore. "Pig—come here! Come here, pig! Pig, I command you!"

"Get back, Azarüb," Charles said, hearing the quiver in his voice but not knowing how to control it. He had grabbed up another rock. "Stay back, or I'll bash your brains in."

Azarüb laughed.

"I think not, Charles." It was still the young voice of Steven, only perverted, corrupted. "I think I'll bash *your* brains in, okay?"

Charles stepped back and looked down at the road. *Hurry, Timothy, hurry. What are you doing down there? Get what you need and get back here* fast!

Marjorie came over to Charles's side and touched his shoulder. "It's not Steven, it's not Steven, *it isn't Steven...*"

"It never was, Marjorie. I'm sorry."

"Oh, God, it's not Steven."

Steven looked right at Marjorie and smiled rather sweetly. "No, I'm not Steven, Marjorie. I'm sorry. But let me introduce myself properly. I do so want to mind my manners now that I'm a guest in *Your Stinking World*—"

With those three words, "Steven" began to change into something else.

The face simply split open as if a machete had *thunked* into its center, and the two flaps fell to the sides. Another face was revealed, a face with some mild human vestiges, but which was mostly alien. As this new face began to thrust out from the old one, Steven's neck began to elongate—not just his neck, but his head, his shoulders, his arms and legs. A low agonized groan issued from the lips of the creature as it continued to transform.

Marjorie and Charles could only stare at the thing standing before them on the hill as it grew and grew and *grew*…

Limbs thickened, new appendages sprouted out of nowhere, a gooey substance poured out of orifices and coated the beast in a sheath of fetid jelly. A tail whipped around in the back, fangs and claws took shape, as well as enormous legs and feet. The eyes were larger, much larger, and the thick lips opened to reveal the full enormity of the horrible mouth.

Charles thought he could hear Timothy down at the roadway, shouting his mystic chants into the air.

But he was afraid his friend might be too late.

CHAPTER FOURTEEN

Somewhere in a fog, in a fantasy, Steven Russell struggled to awaken.

It was like being caught in a bed of gelatin, like being a fly trapped in amber; it was like floating, like being shut inside a dank, dark enclosure and yet spread free across the universe all at the same time. He opened his eyes but closed them quickly. There was too much out there that he didn't want to see. Too much of nothing.

He looked inward: If he tried very hard, he could see out through the eyes of the thing that had absorbed him. He knew its name—knew all its thoughts, just as the thing knew all of Steven's thoughts.

The thing—Azarüb—wanted to kill Marjorie. His wife!

It was all his fault, he knew. He could tell himself a thousand times that it had just been a joke, a childish game, that he'd never intended to hurt anybody and hadn't even really imagined the spell in the nursery would work. But he knew he was ultimately responsible. He'd paid a terrible price—worse than he could even realize—but now innocents, hundreds of innocents, were suffering, and if he were any man at all he would have to fight back. He would have to fight, even though he knew he would incur Azarüb's wrath, that Azarüb could inflict a million agonies on him if he wanted to after-

*ward. That was, if Steven lost. And the odds were great that he
would.*

Still he had to try.

*Steven could not take over the demon's body the way the demon
had taken over his.*

But deep inside the core of the monster, Steven could resist.

Steven Russell could do his part.

*** * ***

Azarüb stood revealed almost in his full glory on top of the
hill. Now that he was in a universe other than his own, he had
made certain adjustments, certain refinements in his form—he
was adaptable—so that he could move about with greater ease
in this gravity, breathe with less trouble in this atmosphere. In
his original form and world, Azarüb would have been difficult for the humans to perceive, to pick out from the landscape
around him. Now he was all too discernible in his singular
unpleasantness. But even though Azarüb had lost one advantage, he had not lost very much of his mind-numbing power.
The three humans would not present much of a challenge.

Azarüb stood nearly ten feet tall. He had metamorphosed
into a vaguely humanoid shape—arms, legs, torso, head—
except that Azarüb also had an enormous tail, six feet long,
that tapered to a sharp end and was already busy slapping at
the ground, digging out chunks of dirt and grass. There was
nothing human about the skin. It was mottled, basically gray-
ish-red in color, with a thick coarse texture like the scaly flesh
of some fish, a thickness to it that probably made it resistant to
the kind of weapons that could easily damage human meat.
An assortment of bumps and protrusions poked out of the
body, and there were also many sunken pits and depressions
that gave off a kind of odorous smoke. There were patches of
skin, inflamed areas, which literally boiled and bubbled as if
the tissue were in a perpetual state of flux, contaminated by a

living, growing rash or infection that would form, heal, and re-form its seeping, suppurating sores continually.

The body itself was strong, muscular, even somewhat lithe and slender. The arms were rather short, with three clawed fingers, but the legs and haunches were large and thick and sturdy. At the bottom of each leg was a heavy broad foot that ended in long piercing tusks that curved downward and dug into the ground. The effect, particularly with that tail, was oddly of a human being bred with a dinosaur, only stranger, uglier, more unearthly, a Tyrannosaurus-man-demon from a world only a lunatic could imagine.

But there was nothing necessarily reptilian about the head. It was massive, almost too big for the body, extremely long, sitting squatly on a fat little neck. It seemed as big as a desk or table, a fleshy elongated wedge with wicked eyes and teeth. The eyes were enormous, lidless, and had no brows; a pure black punctuated by a tiny orange circle in the center. All about the face there were more of those bubbling lavalike rashes. The most terrible thing about the head was the mouth: Its lips were fleshy, blubbery, giant wet chunks of meat that were almost obscenely sensual. Behind those lips were the largest teeth imaginable. What was especially disgusting was that the lips and teeth seemed to be possessed of a life all their own. In the case of the lips, they were alive with twenty score of parasitic maggots that weaved in and out of ugly oily craters and burrows. When Azarüb opened his jaws wide one could see—incredibly—that on each huge tooth there was another mouth, a totally alien orifice that opened and closed unnervingly and made it seem as if the tooth were capable of independent action.

Azarüb also smelled bad, like rotting corpses, animal droppings, spoiled milk, and vomit. A stench like a graveyard, an abattoir, hot stinking garbage in a city in the summertime. The odor was so thick that it, too, seemed to have a separate existence.

Charles knew there was absolutely no hope of holding off this monstrosity until Timothy was ready. Marjorie had nearly fainted at the sight of the beast's transformation, and was now running down the hill screaming at the top of her lungs, completely out of her head. Charles backed away quickly as one of Azarüb's front hands took a swipe at him. The claws hooked onto a button on Charles's shirt and sent it flying, but luckily they made no contact with his flesh. The front paws, in fact, seemed like the demon's weakest, most vulnerable point: too short, really, to strike out at anything, too weak, comparatively speaking, to hold onto anything they managed to grab.

The tail whipped around and slapped hard against Charles's forehead. He cried out in agony, stumbled backward, and fell to the ground. Where the sharp end of the tail had struck, there was a long crimson slash like a razor cut. The injury was throbbing. Charles did as Timothy had done earlier and allowed gravity to snatch him out of the tail's path as it repeatedly whacked down on the spot where he'd been lying a second earlier.

Bruised and battered, Charles picked himself up from the roadside where he had rolled. Marjorie stood by the back of the truck, where Timothy was, her hands covering her mouth. Timothy was standing in the body of the pickup, his book open in his hands, shouting an amalgamation of Latin and an earlier esoteric language into the air. Up on top of the hill the demon bellowed and then came racing down toward them like a sentient, animated steamroller. The clawed feet sank into the ground, *plopped* out of the dirt, leaving behind ghastly footprints like out of a nightmare.

Halfway down the hill the beast stopped all at once; he stood still and swiveled his head to the left, then the right, batted the back of his neck with the tail in a motion that oddly reminded Charles of how a human being would tap his forehead to retrieve a bit of memory. It was as if there were an annoying bee or wasp flying about the demon's head, preoccupying him, annoying him, keeping him from concentrating on his grisly mission.

From the truck, Timothy shouted, "Steven is helping us, too!"

Was that it? Charles wondered. Was Steven's consciousness reasserting itself now that his beloved was in danger? Was he waging a silent invisible war with Azarüb as he had before, keeping the beast so mentally confused that he wasn't able to pounce on the three of them and tear them to shreds, as he certainly wanted to do?

Azarüb grunted, exhaled an almost liquefied breath of oxygen, carbon monoxide, and God only knew what else, and stopped shaking his head and tail. He appeared to be concentrating—concentrating on subjugating Steven's will once again. "Hurry, Tim——hurry!" Charles screamed. Any second the creature might win the battle of wills and he would be on them quicker than they could say his name.

Apparently unable to attack them physically for the nonce —possibly due to Steven's interference—the beast decided to try a different tack. He raised his head skyward and the orange circles in the middle of the blank black eyes began to widen.

"Tim—hurry!"

The skies began to coruscate—black clouds appeared as if from nowhere, and that same hot wind with its unbearable stench wafted across the hillside and across the highway. Lightning crackled menacingly amid the clouds. In a space of several seconds Azarüb had changed the dawn from a quiet, peaceful one with a promise of bright sunshine into a veritable tempest. Rain, which was so hot it burned, fell from the clouds in ever-strengthening intensity. The wind grew stronger and shriller. Timothy grabbed onto Marjorie to steady her and then grabbed onto the truck. Still standing, still reciting, Timothy held his book in one hand, ignored the fluttering pages, and steadied himself by grasping the tailgate. Dawn had turned to twilight; twilight would soon turn to night. Through the dark clouds overhead Charles thought he could see the rising sun sinking, receding back into the earth, but he knew it was illusion. Even Azarüb was not as powerful as all that.

He hoped.

The waves in the sea below splashed with bellicosity and roared into the tiny cove, washing over it and obliterating the small beach in an instant. The tall grasses and weeds bent over in the wind as if at any moment they might be literally torn from the earth. The rain grew stronger and hotter.

"In the truck!" Charles shouted to Marjorie, cupping his hands over his mouth. He led her through the hellish downpour and practically shoved her up into the cab.

Then he went back and hollered through the storm at Timothy, "Get inside—you can finish your ritual *inside.*"

Timothy—the damned fool—shook his head. He motioned for Charles to go back into the truck with Marjorie. Charles had no course but to do as he was told.

Charles rolled up the windows on the truck to keep the hot spattering rainfall from entering. Already there were red spots on his skin where the liquid scorched. He hugged Marjorie to him and kissed away her tears, which did not burn but were both sweet and salty. "I'm sorry," he said. "I'm so sorry."

All at once there came a great crashing sound and the windshield began to take on spidery hairline cracks. Birds, dozens of birds and bats and hawks were coming down out of the sky and smashing into the windows. Already the dead and wounded among them were falling onto the hood and onto the ground. Charles was glad they were safely inside the cab. Then he remembered…

Timothy!

Charles opened the door on the passenger's side and tried to get out, but a huge, fluttering hawk forced him to slam it closed again almost immediately. The hawk continued to pound, scratch, and scrabble against the window. They could hear their winged adversaries clattering on the roof of the cab, battering against the metal like miniature Kamikaze pilots in an effort to bash their way into where their prey was.

Charles knew he had to do something to help Timothy. Under this terrific onslaught he might already be dead or dying. He looked around the cab for something to use as a weapon or at least as cover. Something, *something*. He had torn open the dashboard and thrust his questing fingers into the enclosure, when there was a knock on the window on his side. *Tim!* He saw a pale wretched face covered with blood; a hawk was biting at his ear and a bat was skittering about in his messy red-stained hair.

Charles pushed the door open. He punched the hawk with as much force as he could muster and thought he might have broken a wing. The bat seemed to be more of a nuisance than anything else. It did not resist as he pushed it away. Then a small bird flew into the gap the bat left and tried to peck at him. Since Charles's two hands were busy pulling Timothy into the cab, Charles simply opened his mouth and bit down on the bird's neck as it flapped wildly in his face. He crunched his teeth down, tasting bird blood, and let the crippled or dead animal drop to the floor. He slammed the door and looked Timothy over to gauge the extent of his injuries.

Timothy's face was very badly mutilated, with numerous cuts and larger, more serious wounds. The lobe of one ear was missing, torn away, and there was a long gash in his cheek that would probably require stitches. One eye was so badly swollen and bloodied that for a moment Charles thought that the eyeball itself had been ripped out and all that was left was a hollow socket. Timothy was squinting so badly that Charles couldn't be sure. In several places Timothy's clothes were positively shredded.

Timothy struggled to make himself heard clearly above the avian uproar outside the truck. "Not through, not through," he muttered. "Said the words, spoke the ritual. Almost done.

But I need matches, matches… When birds came, hawks—I dropped my matches."

Charles wanted to tell him to forget all about that now and allow him and Marjorie to wipe the blood away, but he could tell how insistent and desperate his friend was. *They had come this far; they might as well reach a conclusion, whatever it might be.* Charles searched in the glove compartment again and found what Timothy needed, a big, dry packet of matches from an Oriental restaurant in Waikiki. "Here you go. Tell us what we can do to help you. Tell me, Tim!"

"You can get out of this cab…and survive…until I'm through dealing with Azarüb."

"What?"

"You'll only need to stay alive for as long as it takes me to complete the ritual."

"Tim—we can't—"

"I wouldn't ask you, but I need quiet, concentration, a safe place, when I do this. Azarüb will try to stop me. *He must not stop me,* do you hear me, Charles? I must have seclusion—or all of us are *dead!"*

Charles wondered exactly where Azarüb was out in that storm-tossed turmoil of hawks and bats. To go outside now was suicidal enough without knowing from where the demon might spring at them.

Just then a lightning bolt hit the earth about five feet from the truck. The three of them in the cab jumped as one. Charles tried not to panic. Once Azarüb completely mastered his control over the elements they could be incinerated at any moment.

Timothy was more agitated than before. "Get out, *get out* —and God help you. What I have to do now I have to do alone. *Trust me.* It will only be a minute or two."

In the glove compartment Charles found sunglasses that he directed Marjorie to put on so at least her eyes would be protected. He looked out the window and shuddered. "We'll head for that copse of trees across the road," he told Marjorie. She was shivering uncontrollably but she seemed to sense how important it was that they go. "It will all be over soon."

Timothy wheezed in agony and impatience. *"Hurry!"*

The birds seemed to be concentrating on the front of the truck, trying to get in at them through the half-shattered windshield. This was as good a time as any to go. Protecting their faces with old newspapers they had picked off the floor of the cab, Charles and Marjorie stepped out of the driver's side into the maelstrom. Charles turned back to see Timothy lifting the heavy gasoline can onto the seat beside him. In the flurry of bats and birds Charles hadn't noticed he'd brought it with him into the cab a few minutes ago. Gasoline, matches—what was he doing?

Before Charles could come up with the terrible answer, Timothy reached over and slammed down the lock on the door.

"A human sacrifice!" the old man hollered, loud enough to be heard over the storm and through the glass and newspaper. "That's all that will send him back to his realm. A human sacrifice!"

Charles beat frantically against the window. "Tim—no!"

"I've got no choice," Timothy said with a heartbreaking fusion of fatigue and vigor. "I've got no choice at all."

Charles was disconsolate. "No, Tim! *No!*"

Timothy lifted the can of gasoline, opened it, poured it all over himself.

Horrified, Charles saw Timothy lift the match. *God, they had to get away from the truck.*

Totally sick at heart, utterly devastated, Charles took Marjorie through the storm—which served one good purpose in that it battered about the winged servants of Azarüb so much that most of them stayed away from the pair—and headed for the thicket he had seen earlier.

They were halfway there when he heard grunting,

crashing noises to his right and ran faster. More wild boars. And behind them, running up the highway, more people, dozens of people, maddened by Azarüb's power, holding knives and tools and guns and axes. Azarüb was not missing a trick. He was determined to stop Timothy before he could complete the ritual. The earth began to quiver—parts of the cliff high up beyond the demon began to crumble into the sea—and pits and crevices started opening in the earth. One yawned below the truck and the truck began tilting—

"Tim!"

—tilting into a hole that would surely close again and crush the truck and his friend to mush once they were caught inside it. Charles suspected that the matches had fallen from Timothy's hand, that the old man was absurdly crawling on the floor of the cab in search of his death and the earth's salvation…

The landscape was erupting, changing; the hill shimmered and trembled; the waters in the cove below sped up the steep, disintegrating path to the road as if propelled by Neptune's ire. Rocks flew through the air, and the wind and acidic rain churned with fury. An inch-high flood of water from the cove soaked the shifting terrain. Marjorie and Charles took shelter in the trees and hoped the worst of it would pass them by, hoped Steven was still somehow able to fight his possessor in spite of overwhelming evidence to the contrary. Halfway up the hill Azarüb roared.

The truck was still tilting precariously into the crevice. Charles had never felt so helpless. The boars and birds were too confused by the storm to be of much danger. And the people running up the hill looked equally perplexed and disoriented.

There was an explosion inside the cab of the truck, a flash of hungry scarlet, and the whole front of the vehicle burst into flames. The glass in the windshield and windows shot out into space and Charles thought he heard a distant human scream come from the middle of the conflagration, a scream of triumph, regret, and resignation.

*Human sacrifice…the only way…recite the words and spill your own blood…*the only way…

Oh Tim.

Azarüb moved down from the hill in what seemed like one fantastic leap and sprang upon the truck. He lifted the fiery front end of it in his weak hands and formidable jaws almost as if it were a child's toy, and shook it, *shook it,* in a rage.

But it was too late. The whole truck exploded into flames as Azarüb himself caught fire. *All the mouths on all the teeth squealed in unison.*

And then all hell broke loose.

It had taken much energy for Azarüb to pull himself into this world; it would take an equal amount of energy to push him back into his own. As he was wrenched out of this universe, as he screeched and trumpeted his anger, everything in the immediate vicinity was sucked along with him. A whirlpool took shape in the smoke issuing from the crevice where Timothy had died, and truck and monster were yanked into it to disappear without a trace. Now that Azarüb was gone, so, too, was his influence and all vestiges of his existence—but for the whirlpool—and it was a normal dawn on Oahu. The landscape reverted, more or less, to its natural appearance and the frightened wildlife flew or fled back into the forest. The many people on the road woke up as if from out of a trance and, seeing the whirlpool rising up, up from the crevice, began to scream and run for their lives back down from whence they'd come.

Marjorie and Charles held onto a tree trunk and each other and tried not to be wrenched out of this existence by the tug of the wind from the whirlpool. It rose in the air to become a widening cyclone, a magnet drawing rocks, bushes, a few slow-moving birds and bats, into its wake. Skinks and geckos and other small creatures, even boars, were snatched away.

The trees in the copse where Charles and Marjorie hid began to snap and bend; a few saplings were torn out of the earth and sucked into the bright swirling pool of air and fire. The newspapers with which they'd protected their faces had long since been torn away. Marjorie's sunglasses flew off her face and she gasped.

Charles held on, held on as tightly as he could, though the pain and the terror were almost unbearable. It was hard to breathe and he was afraid he might lose consciousness. The tree they were holding onto was slowly being pulled out of the ground...

As it started to go, Charles threw Marjorie instinctively toward another, larger tree and felt himself sliding along the earth, over the highway, and into the terrifying manifestation before him. With a savage outcry and a frenzied, frantic flap of his hands, he was pulled unwillingly from this world of his birth into another he wanted no part of.

* * *

In the demon's universe the funnel opened up into a kind of V-shaped indentation in the "earth" that stretched out into the distance ahead for what seemed like miles, rising, rising, up to a great white light where big flying objects were circling a shining gray sphere. Charles sprawled across the bottom of this ridge where a narrow trickle of blue viscous liquid ran down from the area of the globe. Charles found that he could breathe, but with difficulty. He felt odd—as if he were mildly intoxicated, as if he were seeing every-thing around him through the sides of a muddy fishbowl. He was surprised that he felt no fear.

He got to his feet and immediately looked behind him, looking for the way out back through that whirlpool through which he'd come. He saw only a vague non-anthropomorphic blob of yellow hovering about six feet above the ground. He wondered if he should find a boulder, climb up to the yellow patch, and thrust himself through it.

He thought of Alice in Wonderland and Salvador Dali and surre-alists he had studied years ago. He wondered if he might be dreaming.

He decided to climb up one side of the ridge first; he knew there was something he had to do. Timothy—good, kind Timothy—was dead, had made a noble sacrifice and hopefully saved the world, but what about Steven? Could the young man be brought back to life, back to earth, assuming he was there? And where was Azarüb? He sensed the demon was far away from there, that he had gone some-where in this underworld of his to lick his wounds or the equivalent, or had entered this dimension in an entirely different part of the netherworld altogether. Charles's only thought was of Steven Russell.

He took one step and looked down, felt his first real taste of horror. He had stepped on an eyeball, of sorts, which was embedded in the ground, blinking up at him in dispassion. He lifted his head away from this macabre grotesquerie and saw that there were other eyes dotting both the bottom and sides of the ridge. He resumed his ascent, carefully skirting the dreadful eyeballs whenever they appeared.

He reached the top of the ridge, peered over the embankment.

Saw madness.

There were boulders that appeared to have grimacing lips, plant life—or a kind of plant life—that moved about freely and quickly. He saw no cities as such, only gigantic semi-organic walls, and holes in the walls through which their odd tenants moved. Saw creatures beyond description. It was difficult for him to perceive the dimen-sion's inhabitants—there was so little difference between them and the landscape in which they moved around. It was as if in this strange world the land itself was the lifeform, a multitude of life-forms, "earth" with eyes, rocks with lips, tree-things with teeth. The whole world was alive! *Azarüb was not a peculiarity in this realm; if anything, the demon was ordinary in every sense of the word, even banal.*

Whatever this place was, Charles knew it was not the spirit world—whatever that may have been. Spirits, lost spirits, may have inadvertently wandered into this or other strange dimensions, but this was not the world they normally inhabited. Perhaps the spirit world was only another equally weird dimension someplace else. Not necessarily a comforting thought, to die and wind up keeping company with the likes of Azarüb.

Charles looked to his "left" and saw Steven Russell, naked, draped over a quiet rock-creature that seemed to take no notice of its burden. Charles went over to Steven and saw that he was basically uninjured. He suspected that when Azarüb had been hurled back into this world he had no longer been able to fuse with the earthling; hence, Steven was, in a sense, spat out like a cherry pit from the mouth of a mischievous youngster. He was alive and intact and healthy, and Charles made up his mind that he would take the man home or die in the trying.

Whatever kind of person Steven Russell may have been at one time in his life, whatever his flaws, mistakes, and weaknesses, he had tried his best to redeem himself by fighting back against Azarüb, while most people would have simply given up, given in to a peaceful nonexistence and thereby spared themselves the demon's possible wrath. Azarüb could have taken Steven's soul and inflicted a thousand torments on it, as well as on the man's reconstructed physical form.

But Steven had loved Marjorie and wanted her and others to be spared the many agonies to which Azarüb would have subjected the people of Earth. He was a sensitive man—in some ways like Charles himself or Timothy—who wanted as little suffering in the world as possible.

Charles and Steven said nothing, but could communicate through telepathy as if it were the most natural thing in the world, which in this dimension it probably was. The two of them stumbled back to the rapidly fading patch of shimmering yellow above the ridge. Charles with his brittle old bones climbed on top of Steven's stronger shoulders and dove into the patch, then held out his hand to help lift Steven out after him.

* * *

On Earth it was bright daylight and warm and beautiful. On a boulder not far from their point of reentry, a woman in a pretty yellow *muumuu* sat quietly. It was Marjorie. When she saw the two men appear as if from nowhere, she gasped, held her hand over her heart, and finally smiled as if the sun itself had come to earth and taken up residence inside her. As she walked to their side, Charles, beaming, stepped back and gave Steven a gentle nudge toward his wife. He watched as they stared at each other, as they embraced.

In this world, their world, three days had passed since the final battle with Azarüb.

EPILOGUE

From Charles Emerall's diary:

...no one alive—besides the three of us, and Frank—could ever explain what had happened on Oahu and we knew no one would have believed us. The island will recover in time, but for a while it must mourn its dead and rebuild the devastated areas. It's all being blamed on sudden typhoons, squalls, tidal waves, earthquakes. Oahu looks natural again, the landscape is as it always was, there is no steam and no abnormal crevices at Diamond Head or elsewhere. No one can explain what really happened. Mass hysteria. A series of freak occurrences. People are too wrapped up in their grief to really care. Someday...someday they'll care but there won't be any answers—and so they'll invent them, or blame Pele or "Kanaloa." They'll write books about it—*The Night of Hell on Earth* or something like that; a whole series of investigative accounts and potboiler novels. Not to mention eyewitness reports of residents "as told to" somebody else—*The Night the World Went Mad*. But no one'll really know. No one but we four.

After I disappeared, the whirlpool died away into a mere

frisson in the air, and people and animals completely reverted to normal. Dazed, nearly demented from her ordeal, deeply upset over me and Timothy, Marjorie slowly managed to make her way back to Tim's house, and, from there, to Frank's. (Frank's car had been destroyed along with his truck!) In a disaster, an emergency, all kinds of good, kind people come out of the woodwork, and Frank was only one of many. After a day of rest, Marjorie asked Frank to drive her back to the spot where I'd disappeared, to let her off and return for her at sundown. I will never know if she was waiting for me (Azarüb and her own agitation had made her say those terrible things to me) or for Steven, or what might have happened had I returned without her husband. But she kept a silent vigil on that boulder all that day, hoping against hope that we might reappear, the faithful act of a woman who has nothing to lose...

Of course she must have seen how Steven looked at her, the perplexed uncomprehending look; surely she realized how old she had become in his eyes, how shocked he was at how many years had really passed. It was a bitter irony. All that time he was imprisoned by Azarüb, Steven had not aged *a single day*; he was still a man of twenty-one. (Luckily it was perfectly clear both to me and to Marjorie that this time it *was* Steven and not Azarüb.) Azarüb had imitated Steven at that age because the demon had no conception or understanding of the human aging process. How ironic that when Steven was actually restored to life and to Marjorie he was genuinely no older than the age at which the demon had impersonated him.

But no one spoke of that at that moment. Steven was kind. He was sad and he was disoriented and he was repentant and he was shocked—but he was kind to the woman he loved. It must have been a bitter blow. I was too busy mourning my friend Timothy to pay much attention to Steven Russell and the woman I'd lost. At least Steven had a chance to live life over; how many of us would like *that*? Or rather he had a chance to live his life for the *first* time. He was like a newborn babe, innocent in the ways of the world, a child unleashed forty years out of date in the glittering 1980s. Oh, he has so much to learn.

I discovered that Tim's house was not quite as wrecked as I had imagined; most of our luggage and money were intact. I am writing this now, in his study, as I am staying on for a few weeks as his executor to settle his affairs. It is a most depressing task. Timothy saved every one of us—you and me, everyone—and no one will ever know it.

I can't write about Timothy now; it's too soon.

I had foolishly entertained the notion that Marjorie would come to her senses and let Steven go, let him live his life as a young man, and stay with me in Oahu. (Yes, I think I might live here permanently—if I can dispel the awful memories.) But the night before she left—nearly two weeks later—we had a talk. She told me she realized that things could not be as they *had* been for her and Steven. But she also realized that the man was utterly alone in the world; everyone else he knew was dead—his parents, his friends, his entire generation. She couldn't just abandon him, even if she wanted to—which she didn't. I know something about creating new identities and offered to help create a new one—on paper—for the "late" Steven Russell once they were settled back in Brooklyn. It will not be easy, but I can manage.

Sometimes I lie awake at nights thinking: If he could do it, a foolish boy of twenty-one, what's to prevent someone else from summoning Azarüb—or something worse this time! But I can't dwell on it. First, it's unlikely to happen again. Second, if it's going to happen it's going to happen, and there's not a damned thing you can do about it. Sort of like running into a drunk driver, I suppose.

So after two weeks of resting, talking, getting reacquainted, oriented to their new world and new life together, mourning Timothy and hundreds of others—as well as their dead daughter, Connie, whom Steven had never known—they went back to the mainland. Not as husband and wife, no, but as something closer, something just as deep and precious. Not as husband and wife—they will masquerade as woman and nephew, I think—but as two close friends and companions. They need each other. Steven will be there during the close of Marjorie's life to ease her loneliness. Marjorie will be there to introduce Steven to the 1980s and this bold new world of ours, to be his friend and ease *his* loneliness while he adjusts and meets new people.

But I fear for Steven. Is it the jealous old man inside me, or is the boy really doomed? He is kind, he is sensitive—and he'll find it hard to live with the hundreds of deaths he inadvertently caused on Oahu. Deaths in the storm, deaths at the hands of raging mobs or unearthly monsters. So much death. So much tragedy. Even among the living, people's lives were irreversibly changed, relationships destroyed, altered. Good men raped and murdered their *children*. They awoke as if out of a fog and couldn't even recall *why*. Some of them screamed, some of them jumped out of windows in grief. Good people died and left other good people—people like Marjorie—behind to mourn them for the rest of their lives. The repercussions, legal and moral and emotional, will never end. Never. It hurts to think about it.

True, Azarüb was responsible—not Steven. Yet if Steven had not summoned the demon...he was young, drunk, stupid, desperate—but, in part, he *was* responsible. He might not have known the demon wouldn't stick to their bargain, but he should have realized how treacherous the forces he was dealing with could be...to everyone.

Could you live with that?

I only hope he'll keep himself together for as long as Marjorie is alive and needs him. I know he won't leave her. She's a good woman; she has done no one any harm. And she deserves some happiness. Let them stay in their harbor of love for as long as they can—they'll have precious little else.

But afterward—who can say? I don't know how it will all work out. It won't be easy—not for either of them.

I'll miss Marjorie. I had barely gotten to know her. I thought she could have been my...friend.

For her sake, for the sake of that lonely, suffering woman whose life was always so bleak and hopeless:

I'm glad I brought him back.

ABOUT THE AUTHOR

William Schoell is the author of over 35 books, including celebrity biographies, books for young adults, tomes on the performing arts and popular culture, and novels, especially in the thriller-horror genre. He has been a radio producer and talk show host, worked for Columbia Pictures, is an activist and blogger, and playwright.

Schoell is a native New Yorker, born in Manhattan, where he resides.

www.ingramcontent.com/pod-product-compliance
Lightning Source LLC
Chambersburg PA
CBHW011151310726
48973CB00010B/2857